The man was an interesting contradiction.

Maybe that's why Debra kept wondering about him.
Why her eyes kept finding him. Why he stayed at the
edges of her mind. Jonah seemed different from most
men she knew.

In the corporate world, she dealt with power-hungry
men, or men concerned with wearing the right suit,
driving the right car and having the right title on
their business cards. Men like Mia's father. Someone
who'd made promises he couldn't keep, or wasn't
man enough to keep.

Jonah was a man who knew how to keep his promises
and honor his commitments.

* * *

Books by Jillian Hart

Love Inspired

Heaven Sent #143
*His Hometown Girl #180
A Love Worth Waiting For #203
Heaven Knows #212
*The Sweetest Gift #243
*Heart and Soul #251
*Almost Heaven #260
*Holiday Homecoming #272
*Sweet Blessings #295
For the Twins' Sake #308
*Heaven's Touch #315
*Blessed Vows #327
*A Handful of Heaven #335
*A Soldier for Christmas #367
*Precious Blessings #383
*Every Kind of Heaven #387
*Everyday Blessings #400
*A McKaslin Homecoming #403
A Holiday To Remember #424

*The McKaslin Clan

JILLIAN HART

makes her home in Washington State, where she has lived most of her life. When Jillian is not hard at work on her next story, she loves to read, go to lunch with her friends and spend quiet evenings with her family.

A Holiday To Remember
Jillian Hart

Steeple
Hill®

Published by Steeple Hill Books™

Special thanks and acknowledgment are given to
Jillian Hart for her contribution to the
A TINY BLESSINGS TALE miniseries.

STEEPLE HILL BOOKS

Steeple
Hill®

ISBN-13: 978-0-373-81338-4
ISBN-10:   0-373-81338-4

A HOLIDAY TO REMEMBER

www.SteepleHill.com

Printed in U.S.A.

My purpose is that they may be encouraged
in heart and united in love.
—*Colossians* 2:2

Chapter One

"Mom, are you even listening to me?"

"Sure I am, kid." Debra Cunningham Watson was too busy navigating her SUV down the small Virginia town's unfamiliar and icy streets to do more than shoot a quick glance in her thirteen-year-old daughter's direction. "I'm just trying not to crash into the car in front of us."

Did they have to hit the noon-hour rush? Things had not been going according to plan for this entire trip, which was why they were running late. The long line of slow-moving traffic through the town's main street didn't help. Nor did the knowledge that the appointment she had to keep was a personal one—meeting with Ben Cavanaugh, the half brother she didn't know she had until six months ago. Talk about being thrown for a loop. She still couldn't quite believe it.

"Mom, aren't the decorations *awesome?*"

Mia was at the age where everything was either awesome or tragic. Since the line of cars ahead of her had stopped inching forward due to a red light, Debra relaxed back into the leather seat, took her eyes from the road and considered her daughter. Talk about high hopes. Meeting her cousins from Ben's side of the family, along with his wife, her new aunt, was about all Mia could talk about during the morning-long drive on wintry roads from their home near Baltimore.

Mia leaned against the restraint of her seat belt to point across the dash. "Is that like the biggest Christmas tree ever? They're using the fire truck's ladder. Look!"

"So I see." Debra hadn't noticed, she'd been too busy stressing over the compact snow and ice on the road. But since the traffic was still stopped, she took a moment to scan up the street, where two city workers were mounting Christmas lights in the shapes of giant candy canes and Christmas stars and silver bells on the utility poles.

Beyond the block of quaint shop-lined street, she spotted a city park, where snow blanketed a stretch of grass and mantled picture-perfect evergreens. In the center of the square was an enormous spruce, probably as old as the town itself, long graceful boughs holding up strings of fat, lit bulbs. What would it be like to live in such a postcard-perfect place?

Impossible, that's what. It was like a Currier & Ives scene, with the morning's snowfall fresh on the ground and crisping the roofs and awnings and trees along the row of shops. It could even make someone as driven as she was wish for a quieter life. Then again, a quieter life often came with a less impressive paycheck, and that meant no Chesapeake Bay-view home and no prestigious private school for Mia. No top-of-the-line luxury SUV.

And it wasn't only material things at stake, Debra thought with a heavy heart as the traffic began to creep forward and she eased her foot back onto the gas pedal. There were the family obligations to consider. Obligations to those living and those gone.

Debra's throat ached with sorrow and she forced down the grief that still felt too immense to handle. It had not been easy to lose her mother. To make it all worse, coming to this adorable little town was like digging up all that grief and hurt and confusion and feeling it anew.

But not for Mia. No, learning about Ben had

seemed to help the girl with her burden of grief, for she and her grandmother had been tight. Practically joined at the hip. Mia was lit up as she took in every detail. "Mom! Don't you see it? It's a sign."

Uh-oh, here we go again, Debra thought. "You mean, the sign that says, Welcome to Chestnut Grove?" She couldn't help but tease a little because she knew it would make her daughter smile or at least roll her eyes in the way of teenagers everywhere. But did it divert Mia? Not a chance.

"Mom, really. You know I meant a sign from heaven, not a physical signpost." Mia pursed her lips in ladylike disapproval, thirteen going on forty-three. "This sign can only mean one thing."

"I'm afraid to ask what."

"That God is about to answer my deepest, most secret prayer."

There she went talking about God again. It took all Debra's effort to snap her mouth shut and keep it that way. Thankfully, the street she needed to turn left onto came into view and she pulled the SUV into the icy turn lane. When she eased onto the brakes, the vehicle skidded to a safe stop. "If I had a prayer, it would be to arrive at Ben's business in one piece."

"Do you know what your problem is, Mom?"

"I'm afraid to know the answer to that, too."

"You don't believe in the power of prayer."

Where had she heard this exact phrase before? Oh, yes, constantly, the entire time she was growing up. Debra didn't know if she believed in heaven anymore, but she knew beyond a doubt that her mother had. And if her mother were there, then surely she would be looking down rejoicing in the fact that her granddaughter was carrying on her life's work to save as many people as possible, especially Debra.

Resigned, Debra turned at the break in traffic and crept through the intersection. The temperature was dropping, confirmed by the gauge on the dash and the fact that the passenger compartment felt colder. Snow clouds hung overhead, gathering momentum. With any luck, they'd finish seeing Ben and be able to get back to the bed-and-breakfast before more of the white stuff fell. Debra turned up the heater.

"I'll have you know that prayer works." Mia gave her curly brown hair a flip. "I know it does because we're here in Chestnut Grove right now. Together. It's proof."

"We're here because we agreed to meet Ben."

"But we're meeting Ben because I prayed for more family to love and God answered me. He had to take Grandmother Millie from us, but He saw fit to give us Ben."

How did she tell Mia that God and prayers had nothing to do with it? That a carpenter had been renovating a wall in some mansion here in this town, and had discovered original birth certificates and records of adoptions that had been falsified. Ben Cavanaugh's birth information had been part of those discovered records and that's how he had found them.

It was not God's handiwork, she thought sensibly, but the result of someone renovating a house. Debra was on her way to touch bases with her half brother not because of some grand design by God. Really. It was happenstance—mere chance—that they'd even learned about Ben at all. That was why they were here. The *only* reason they were here.

But she didn't say that to Mia, not when she knew those words would dampen her daughter's happiness. Debra cut her eyes from the road long enough to take in Mia's dear face. She had a light scattering of freckles across her perfect nose and a peaches-and-cream complexion. Dimples bracketed her bright smile, and she radiated hope and life.

When was the last time she saw her daughter so bubbly? Her dark eyes glinted with a joyful brightness that had been missing since, well, Debra realized with a heavy heart, since her mom's passing. There was no way she would take an ounce of Mia's hope away, but larger questions had plagued her since all of this came to light.

What if it was a mistake getting involved with Ben and his family? They were strangers. They'd only met Ben once, when he'd made a short trip to Maryland to meet them. He'd been nice—but so were a lot of people on the surface. What if once his curiosity about them was satisfied, Ben cut off all ties? What would that do to Mia?

Debra had plenty of other doubts and concerns, but that was the greatest one. Which was why her stomach was becoming a tighter knot with every click of the odometer. She checked the cross street at the corner signpost adorned with Christmas lights and realized they were a block away. One more block and they would come face to face with Ben. With all her uncertainties and questions and doubts.

Don't think about them now, Debra, she told herself. She was here for Mia. To make this a good experience for her daughter. Goodness knew, they'd had enough bad ones lately and it was taking its toll.

"A Christian bookstore, Mom! Cool. We'll have to stop there later, promise?" Mia seemed enchanted by the town's streets, which did have a certain charm. "Oh, and that's a school. A *junior high*. That would be better any day than my yucky school."

"The Stanton School is one of the best in the country." And also their biggest source of conflict, Debra thought, but decided to keep her tone light. "I went there. Your aunt Lydia went there. Your grandmother Millie went there."

"I know." Mia rolled her eyes. "I'm a Cunningham *and* a Watson. There would be nowhere else I could possibly go. Family tradition is *so-oo* important."

Normally Debra would comment on the sarcasm, but this wasn't the time. She had enough on her mind, and did she dare break Mia's wonderful good mood? Absolutely not. It had actually lasted all morning long. A record for recent times. Debra pulled the SUV to a stop in front of Cavanaugh's Carpentry and cut the engine.

"We're here! I can't stand it." Mia hit the seat-belt release. "I'm *so* excited. I'm glad we're seeing Uncle Ben and all, but I don't know if I can wait much longer to meet Aunt Leah and Cousin Olivia and baby Joseph."

"You'll manage." Before Debra could pull the keys from the ignition, Mia was already out the door, the frigid gusts of wind tangling her hair and blowing her coat open. Her hand-knit, designer sweater might be made of wool, but it was hardly protection against this kind of weather. "Zip up and pull on your hood, sweetie."

"I'm too happy to feel cold!" Mia argued, but did as she was told in an absentminded way, gawking about as if this were the most remarkable place on earth.

As the passenger door slammed shut, Debra buttoned her wool peacoat and wrapped a scarf over her head. In the two moments it took for her to pull her warmest gloves from the console, Mia had circled around and was opening the driver's door for her.

"Mom! Hurry up! You're taking *forever.*"

Debra couldn't help laughing just a little. It helped with the mounting worries that just kept plaguing her. So much could go wrong.

Then again, maybe that only meant there were a lot of things to go right. After all, she'd already met her half brother once, right? Ben was a nice man—it was hard not to like him. Although months had passed since she'd found out this shocking news, she still couldn't quite grasp it. Her mind understood it, but her heart could not accept it.

"Snowflakes!" Mia held out her mittened hand, palm up, to let the first airy, dizzying flakes of snow land. "Mom, it's a sign."

"How is that possible?" She climbed down from the seat and closed the door. "You think everything is a sign."

"That's 'cause everything *is* a sign. God is everywhere, watching over us. Grandmother Millie always said that and it's true. See?"

It looked like there would be no escaping Grandmother Millie or her religious influence on Mia—and although these things were thorns in her side, Debra decided to ignore the sting. She'd made a promise to her daughter and considering the difficulties they'd had lately, she wanted to put her best effort into this trip, into bringing them closer together.

"They are lovely," Debra said of the snowflakes. If one had an overactive imagination, like Mia, then, Debra conceded, the crisp, lovely fragile flakes *could* look like a sign of good things to come.

"Not lovely, Mom. Perfect." A gust of wind

threw her hood back and Mia twirled, letting the snowflakes catch in her cloud of soft brown hair. "Everything's gonna be perfect. I just *know* it. This is gonna be a holiday to remember."

"I hope so, sweet pea."

If she were a religious woman, Debra would pray for it to be true. But why put her energies into something so unproven? Faith was like those snowflakes on the wind, dizzily falling where the air currents took them. She could catch one on the tip of her fingers if she wanted to, but what good would it do? It would melt away and she'd be left with nothing.

Besides, she had learned to rely on herself and nothing had been the same since Mom's passing. Now, with Ben, it could never go back to the way things were. Even the memory of her family—of her mother—was tarnished.

She beeped the door locked as the snowflakes swirled around her, not at all surprised to hear the thump of her daughter's fashionable boots on the shoveled front step.

The wind gusted, catching the fringe of her scarf and the hem of her coat. It felt like a touch against her face, turning her gently leftward. Her gaze aligned perfectly with a large window, offering a view inside the carpenter's workshop where a lone man was kneeling in a fall of soft gray daylight. Broad of shoulder, humble in appearance and deeply masculine, the man worked with his head bent, carefully brushing sandpaper over a corner of something made of wood—his big body blocked any view of it.

Who is he? The question filled her mind and stilled all the worries and cautions in her heart. She forgot to take a step forward and simply stood rooted in place with the snowflakes sifting through the icy air like pure sugar, unable to take her eyes off the man. He was so big and rugged looking, he could have been made of steel.

Not that she was prone to noticing men or how they were built. Maybe it wasn't him that held her attention at all, she rationalized. Perhaps what caught her attention was the unlikely contrast between the intimidating-looking linebacker of a man working so patiently at his craft. It seemed like a paradox.

"Mom?" Mia had retraced her steps to see what had captured her mother's attention. "That's not Uncle Ben. Who is it?"

"I don't know. Probably one of his employees."

Before she could move, the woodworker stiffened, as if he sensed her gaze. The breath left her lungs when he suddenly stood, all six feet of him, and stared back at her. He was pure silhouette, backlit by the faint light spilling from above. Caught between darkness and light he looked almost unreal, a shadowed form and nothing more.

Even before he took a step forward and moved into the light, Debra felt the power of his protective spirit; how silly was that? She wasn't given to flights of fancy. She didn't have the luxury of it as a hardworking single mom.

He gestured to the side of the building, not the front door, and Mia took off at a fast clip, galloping toward what appeared to be a side door. It swung open and there he was, the man in flesh and bone, with thick brown hair, dark eyes and a strong, ruggedly handsome face. He wore a plain navy blue thermal Henley and sawdust-covered jeans.

The look of him didn't come as a surprise. If she were to describe him in a single word, it would be *intimidating*.

"Who are you?" Mia demanded. "I'm here to see my uncle Ben."

"You must be Mia. I'm Jonah Fraser. And you—" Jonah lifted his gaze to hers. His dark eyes focused on her with frank scrutiny. "You're Debra. The half sister."

"Yes, although that's a new title for me."

He continued to study her stoically. He was just this side of frightening, Debra thought, because he felt so remote. His size alone was daunting, but he said nothing else. Apparently he was a man of few words.

Was he the withdrawn, quiet type? Or simply unfriendly? No, not unfriendly, she decided as he gestured with one big hand toward the door. He was very self-controlled.

"Come in," he said. "Ben's not—"

"He isn't here?" Mia had a good view through the doorway as she skidded to a stop in front of Jonah Fraser. "But we came all this way and he promised. He said he'd have plans of what we're gonna do next and everything."

So, Ben was a no-show.

I feared this might happen, Debra bit her lip to keep the words to herself. Hadn't she almost expected that Ben would let down Mia and then where would she be? Then again, maybe she was expecting the worst.

She stepped forward to lay her hand on her daughter's slim shoulder. "We are about an hour late. I almost called first from the bed-and-breakfast, but Ben had left a message with the manager just to head straight over."

"Did he give up waiting for us?" Mia asked, her voice trembling.

"No." Kindness flickered in Jonah's eyes, which were darkly inscrutable. "An emergency call came in and he had to go out."

"Will he be back?" Mia asked, distressed.

"He promised."

Debra didn't want to notice the steady warmth in Jonah Fraser's eyes or the subtle but unmistakable calm. Although he was physically intimidating, she felt intensely safe. And she couldn't rightly say why. "Do you know if Ben will be long? We could head back to our room and wait for him."

"No need." He took a step, leading the way, and the strong line of his shoulders dipped slightly as he drew his right leg forward.

He was limping. And seriously. He was athletic enough that he compensated fairly well, but his wasn't the kind of limp one might have with a sprained ankle. No, Jonah moved as if he'd been seriously wounded. She worked with a man who'd had a severe car accident and even years later, walked similarly. Had something like that happened to Jonah?

He held the door and closed it after them, stiffly polite. "Go through that door. You'll be more comfortable in there."

She imagined he'd feel more comfortable, too. She untied her scarf and snowflakes tumbled from the wool to the floor between them. Jonah said nothing, leaving silence to fill the space. She didn't know what to say to this man who looked like he was made of steel on the inside, too. He certainly didn't say much.

Which was a change from most men she knew. She realized she was staring at him a little too openly and her face heated. Really, what was wrong with her? Was this a sign she was losing it completely? She'd been under a lot of strain lately, but she wasn't one to openly study a man, as if she were interested....

Really, she was not interested in another man who would only let her down. She turned to take Mia's coat and realized the girl had wandered off toward a maze of machines in the middle of the shop, and some had sharp-looking blades. "Mia, don't snoop. Come back here."

"But, Mom, you gotta see this! It's *awesome*."

It was the wonder in Mia's voice that drew Debra forward, to see over a huge angular and very technical-looking saw to a lone crib in the later stages of construction. Without stain or varnish, without polish or even all of its pieces, the crib was beautiful. It stood in the sift of light from a roof window directly overhead and looked like something out of a dream, diffused with light.

As Debra stepped closer, she saw the careful scrollwork and the intricate hand carving that was sheer perfection. She ran her fingertip over the smooth-as-glass texture, feeling awe sift through her like the snowflakes outside.

The time and patience it must take to do such beautiful work, she couldn't imagine. It was delicate and fragile and storybook beautiful, but what really mystified her was the man who'd made it.

The reticent, brawny Jonah Fraser had done *this*.

Chapter Two

Jonah Fraser stirred the contents of the last hot-chocolate package into the coffee cup, watching the tiny white marshmallows swirl in the whirlpool created by the spoon. He held his emotions still as he kept Debra Cunningham Watson, of the publishing empire, in his peripheral vision.

Ben had talked about her and, since Ben was more than his employer but a close friend, he felt that he had some stake in this. Ben had been glad to learn the identity of his birth mother and that while she had sadly passed away, he had three other half siblings to get to know. Debra was the oldest of the Watson clan and she was about what he expected.

Ben had glossed over the details, but Jonah could read between the lines. She had that tight-lipped reserve he'd seen before from old-money families. He knew she was a big executive, a vice president or something. Everything about her shouted privilege, from her sleek brown locks to her perfect skin and smile to the upscale designer clothes she wore. Conservative black wool and trendy winter boots. Yep, she definitely looked like the type of woman who had an MBA from Harvard.

Jonah removed the spoon from the cup. He kept Debra Watson in his sight while he grabbed the two chipped mugs by the handles and headed their way. A few things about her puzzled him. One, her chin-up, lips-pursed attitude had softened as she studied the crib. That told him her manner was more facade and habit, it was easy to see she wasn't as icy as she first seemed.

The second thing that surprised him was the age of the daughter. Twelve or thirteen, he guessed. Ben had mentioned the girl, but not her age, not that Jonah could recall, and it made him wonder what had gone on there. Debra must have gotten married young and divorced. That was his guess, anyway.

"Wow, this is so cool." Mia was all cheerful exuberance as she circled the crib. "Are you, like, *making* this? I mean, you're just making it all by yourself?"

"Yep. With wood and tools and everything."

"It's so cool!"

"Thanks." He took one look at the girl's innocent excitement and suddenly the memory of other children in another country hit him like a flash flood. *Stay in the present, bud,* he told himself, fighting the flashback. He locked down the doors on his heart before his sorrow and guilt could overtake him and bolted those doors good.

He set both cups down on the nearby worktable that stood between them. "Hot chocolate with minimarshmallows. I hope that's okay."

"Thanks!" The kid lit up. She was easily thrilled. Anyone could see she'd been raised with care and love. And manners, because she grabbed both cups and took one to her mother. To the woman who was staring at him as if he'd sprouted antennae and turned martian green.

Great. He often had that effect on women who didn't know him. He'd experienced this before. The more dainty and proper and upper-crust the lady, the more likely she was to be put off by the sheer size of him.

He *was* a big guy, and he'd been told he looked fairly fierce. He couldn't argue with that—a recon marine was about as tough of a warrior as it was possible to be. He knew the stain of what he'd accomplished and failed to accomplish as a marine in Iraq clung to him like residue. He often wondered if it somehow put other people off.

"Thank you." The woman—Debra—had taken a step back as if she were intimidated and took a dainty sip of the hot chocolate. Somehow she was able to avoid the marshmallow fluff that stained her daughter's mouth. The girl had come around the worktable to stare openly at him, while the woman—Debra—was studying the crib.

So he took a moment to study her. Ben's half sister. He couldn't see it at first. But as she stepped into the softer daylight from the roof windows, it became more evident in the simple straight dignity of her nose, which wasn't too small or big, and in the manner that she held her head just so while she thought. Snowflakes were melting in the silk of her hair and on the collar of her fancy fur-lined coat.

"This is lovely." She gave him a polite smile. "You are a very talented woodworker."

A blush heated his face. He shrugged one shoulder. "I try."

"And modest, too. That's a change from the men I've been around lately."

"Can't be much of a man if he isn't humble."

"Exactly." She smiled; it was an honest smile.

For a moment he saw past the polite veneer and cool distance into something brighter. Maybe it was just a trick of the gray light from above or his falling blood sugar. He'd delayed his lunch hour so he could be here for Ben's half sister. More importantly, he'd wanted to meet this woman. He was protective of his good friend.

"I imagine it was hard finding out that you have an older brother," he heard himself saying.

"You have no idea." She said it kindly but as if there was more to it. "I was just as shocked to learn of Ben, as Ben was to learn he was related to us. I'm still trying to adjust. It's strange going from being the oldest to the second out of the blue."

There was pain there, Jonah realized, a pain she quickly battled down. Okay, he had sympathy for that. He understood inner pain— it haunted him every moment of every day, and he didn't know what to say to her.

She broke the silence, gesturing toward the crib. "Is this for Ben's baby, Joseph?"

"No, this is for some good friends of mine, and of Ben's, too. Ross and Kelly Van Zandt's baby boy. He arrived a little earlier than expected."

"Is that the same Kelly from the adoption agency? Ben mentioned her." Debra glanced at her daughter, who was still staring at him. "Mia, where are your manners?"

"It's okay," he added quickly, wondering if the waiflike girl was a little scared of him. She wouldn't be the first. "Are you wondering why I'm so big? God made me this way so I could serve His purpose."

"What purpose?" Mia asked, wide-eyed. "Are you a Christian, too? Which church do you go to?"

She looked up at him with curiosity in her big innocent eyes, her cupid's face wreathed with expectation. Cute kid, obviously sheltered and privileged and well cared for, just as a child should be. He battled down images of the world he'd seen—not good images, where children were not so safe and protected. He noticed the gold chain and cross at her throat. "Yes, I'm a Christian. I belong to the Chestnut Grove Community Church."

"That pretty one with the big steeple that looks like it belongs in a storybook?"

"That's the one."

"Wow."

"Yes, wow." Debra squelched an inner groan. Irrepressible Mia felt that everyone should be saved. It was a nice sentiment, but unrealistic. She'd taken so many hard blows lately between her mom's passing and then over the truth about her mom's past, these days she was putting faith in God right up there on the shelf with her thoughts about Santa Claus. Nice, but not relevant to her life.

That sounded harsh, but she was a grown woman who'd gotten where she was with hard work, determination and having to face adult responsibilities without a lot of help.

Okay, there she went again when she had vowed to focus on Mia and the trip. Time for a change in subject. "Mia, come on. Let's wait in the reception area and let Mr. Fraser get back to his work. I'm sure we're inconveniencing him."

"But, Mom!" Mia's jaw dropped in utter disbelief. "Can't you see we're talking about God?"

"I thought you were about to pry into Mr. Fraser's personal life and make sure he's really a Christian, the way you did with the gas-station attendant this morning. The way you do with everyone you meet."

To her surprise, the big, stony Mr. Fraser smiled. He wasn't quite as fearsome when he did. The granite line of his square jaw softened and his hard mouth that could have been sculpted from stone warmed into a handsome smile. He had straight, even white teeth and a sincerity that made him striking.

She felt a frisson of interest as pure as the snowflakes fluttering down from the heavens. This man perplexed her. He was apparently part weightlifter and part legend with an artist's soul.

"Call me Jonah," he said. "When I hear *Mr. Fraser,* I think my dad is standing behind me. Besides, the little lady isn't inconveniencing me or prying."

"You truly are a kind man to say so," Debra found herself saying. "Mia has better manners than that—"

"*Reverend* Fraser is your dad?" Mia interrupted, in direct contradiction.

What was a mother to do? Mia had a strong spirit and a stubborn streak, not unlike herself at that age. Debra caught Mr. Fraser's—Jonah's—gaze and watched his smile deepen until it warmed the cool depths of his eyes.

He was definitely a different kind of man than she was used to being around, but suddenly she was no longer intimidated by the rugged strength of him. Whatever else Jonah Fraser may be, she bet he was a teddy bear at heart because he turned patiently to Mia and his manner was genuinely kind. "Why don't you come to Sunday service and I'll introduce you to him? At least, I'm guessing that you'll be attending with Ben and his family."

"Ye-ah." Mia rolled her eyes heavenward as if there couldn't possibly be any other answer, so why did he bother asking?

It seemed like everywhere she turned, there was the conflict over Mia's faith—and Debra's lack of conviction. But what could she say to such a kindly meant invitation? "We'll talk about Sunday later, Mia."

"Mo-om!"

"We were going to take this visit one day at a time, remember?" Time for another change in topic. The trouble was, why did her first thoughts turn to Jonah and finding out more about him? "How long have you been making such beautiful furniture?"

"Oh, I've always been fairly handy." He eased forward, his shoulder dipping slightly to compensate for his limp. "I've always worked with wood in one way or another—"

Mia broke in. "You didn't want to be a minister like your dad?"

Debra inwardly cringed. Was Mia wound up today or what? "Mia, you know better than to interrupt."

"It's all right." Jonah's baritone rang with patience and good humor as he drew up a metal stool and eased his big frame onto it. "I thought very seriously about joining the ministry, but I didn't feel a real calling to do it. There's another reason, too. I like to write, but I'm not so good with talking in front of a crowd. If I had to talk to a congregation, I'd stammer and forget my sermon, and my looking like a fool wouldn't help anyone."

There was something innately noble about him. She could see it now, as his quiet tough-guy manner softened a bit. He radiated a subtle but unmistakable strength of character.

Drawn to him, Debra came closer and rested the hot mug on the table. She did want to know more about this man. Something told her he was interesting. His combination of brawny toughness and shy woodworker intrigued her. "You look like a man who could never be a fool."

"Well, I suppose you mean that as a compliment and I thank you for it, but I've made mistakes like anyone else. Maybe more than most." Sadness, or maybe it was regret, shadowed his expressive eyes. His face turned stony. "I wound up following a calling I was more suited to rather than following my dad's path."

"You have more courage than I did at the

time. Instead of following my dreams or my calling, I followed my mother's path in life. Same college, graduate school and then I went to work for my family's company."

"There's no shame in that, none at all. Ben tells me that you're in publishing?"

"Yes." Was it her imagination or was he intentionally changing the subject? Well, she could do that, too. "Do you regret not following your father's path? Or are you content with your choices?"

"Some days, yes. Some days, no." His easiness vanished and he looked sad again. "Life never turns out the way you expect."

"Or want." They apparently had that in common. She felt so many emotions begin to work their way into words; emotions she'd not really taken out to examine in a good long time. "We get caught up in what we should do. What we ought to be. What we mean to do. It never turns out the way you intend."

"That's why I love my job here, working at building things. It's nothing like real life with tragedy and things you can never reconcile. When I sit down to make a piece of furniture, there's only the doing of it. The feel of the wood in my hands, rough at first, then the shaping of it, the sanding and carving and finishing. If it doesn't come out as I intended, nine times out of ten it comes out better."

"I wish life could be that way."

"Me, too."

Jonah wondered if she had any idea how transparent she was at that moment. Her icy career woman's veneer was down and the wintry daylight burnished her with a silver glow. He could see the longing in her eyes for something—he didn't know her at all, so he couldn't guess at what that might be—before her practical side won over and the moment was gone.

It was a puzzle what a put-together woman like Debra, who looked like she had it going on, would have to regret in life. Ben hadn't mentioned if Debra had a husband. Jonah didn't see a wedding ring on her slender, manicured hands. Had she suffered through a divorce? A painful marriage?

It still amazed him that she didn't look old enough to have a teenage daughter. She looked so young herself. Her heart-shaped face was luminous, reminding him of the female leads in those black-and-white movies—so radiant and serene, peaceful and timeless. What could a woman with so much going for her have to regret?

He thought of his own failures, of the men

he'd failed. The remembrance settled like a weight on his soul. What would she think of him if she knew?

"Mom! Mom!" The girl had moved to the far side of the crib, kneeling down to inspect the turned legs. "I've got the best idea ever."

Debra smiled and it only made her lovelier. "I live in fear of your best ideas."

"But this really is the best one! You gotta come look. Please?"

Debra pushed away from the table. "I'm going to admire your handiwork again. How long does it take for you to build something like this, from start to finish?"

"As long as it takes to do it right."

"You're not a man who bills by the hour?"

"Only by the job." What else could he say to that? He supposed a woman with her business background had a clear understanding of profit margins and whatnot, but he didn't care so much. How did he say it was the reward of the job well done and to the best of his ability? It was something no one could pay him for. It was something he didn't know how to explain.

Mia studied him over the top of the frame. "Do you make other stuff, too? Like beds?"

"Sure. I finished a bedroom set before this."

"You mean, a bed and a dresser? Really?"

"Unbelievable, but true."

Mia clasped her hands as if in prayer. "Could you make one for me? Can he, Mom? Please, please, *please?*"

I should have seen this coming, Debra thought as she tugged at her jacket cuffs, straightening them, giving her a chance to think. Saying no was on the tip of her tongue—they'd talked about redoing Mia's room, but that was before she went away to school. Lately, they'd had bigger topics to discuss, like meeting Ben for the first time, the changes in their family and the changes in what they knew to be true about her mother. All the issues that seemed to tear them apart even further. The bedroom remodel had been pushed onto the back burner.

Mia's radar apparently was sensing weakness because she abandoned the lovely crib to grab hold of Debra's hand. "*Please?* You said you'd think about new stuff for my room and that was a long time ago. I've been patient and everything."

"I know, sweet pea. We did talk about new furniture—"

Before she could say a single word more, Mia gave a squeal of delight. "Yes! Oh, thank you, thank you, thank you!"

Across the scuffed worktable, Jonah was grinning at her. Grinning. As if he found this to be highly amusing. It was an all-out, full-scale smile that knocked her socks off, she believed the term went. She'd never quite experienced such a reaction before. She was certain that her toes were at least tingling as the big man met her gaze.

For a fraction of a moment, it felt as if the world stopped spinning. As if time stood still. She couldn't explain it and before she could analyze it, Jonah tore his gaze away and pulled out a battered three-ring binder from a nearby shelf. As if nothing had happened between them, as if nothing had changed whatsoever, he went to work thumbing through the binder, holding it open in one big hand. With an economy of movement, he slipped the binder onto the table between them.

"Here are a few snapshots of a bedroom set I've done in the same pattern." He gazed at her with a knowing look, as if he knew she'd already made up her mind to get the entire set.

Him leaning over the table to show her the page made her draw closer. So close, with only the book separating them, she could see that his eyes, which appeared black from a distance, were really a striking dark brown with flecks of gold. This close, she could see that a faint shadow clung to his jaw as if he hadn't shaved that morning. He smelled like soap and he looked even more invincible. The strong presence that he projected intensified, and she could see the rapid beat of his pulse in his neck. There was no doubt about it, if she'd come across this man in an abandoned alley, her first reaction would be alarm. But down deep, she knew on an instinctive level that Jonah Fraser was all man, and he was a very good one.

Why on earth was she noticing the furniture maker and not the furniture? What had come over her? Debra mentally shook herself and forced her gaze down to the plastic-covered pages where snapshots, neatly taken, displayed a breathtaking cherrywood bedroom set. Obliviously hand tooled to perfection.

"Mia, why don't you come look at this?" The words tumbling out of her mouth didn't sound like hers at all. This wasn't like her. Why? She took a step back and to the side as her daughter approached. "This should be your decision, kid. This will be your furniture for a long time to come."

"Wow! Cool, Mom." Mia bounced against the table.

Now, if only she could focus on the lovely furniture they were about to buy instead of the man towering over her. Goodness, she hadn't been intrigued by a man romantically since Mia's father had walked out on her. That was the day she'd closed the door to her heart and locked it for good—or for at least until Mia was grown. So what was going on?

Quiet Jonah had opened that door to her feelings, she realized. Impossibly, in a matter of moments, he'd done what no other man had been able to do for the last thirteen years.

Suddenly she realized it was silent and that both Mia and Jonah were staring at her expectantly. Had she missed something? Her mind scrambled to try to figure out what it could have been. The last thing she remembered was the furniture.

It wasn't like her to check out like that or to notice a man—any man—so strongly that she lost track of what was going on around her.

"You don't like the sleigh bed?" Mia asked in distress.

"Oh, baby, I think it's lovely." Okay, she was back on track. She brushed her fingertip across the plastic photo-sleeve page, trying to ignore Jonah's gaze, a brush against the side of her face.

Had he guessed that she was curious about him? How embarrassing. There was no way she could look him in the eye now. She stared hard at the page and hoped beyond hope her voice would sound normal—or at least not so vulnerable.

"This is truly an incredible set. You do amazing work, Jonah."

"Everything I do is custom. If you want a different piece than I've got here, I'll sketch something up for you. You name it, I'll build it."

He had the warmest baritone, as cozy in sound as a fire in a hearth, inviting you closer. Debra truly wished she wasn't affected.

Mia planted her elbows on the table. "And, like, maybe a desk, huh, Jonah?"

His fathomless gaze softened. "What kind? How 'bout a lady's writing desk? Good for studying or using your computer but looks pretty, too. Won't take up a lot of room."

"Yes!" Mia put on her most innocent look. "I can have that, too, right, Mom?"

"Right." Fighting hard to keep her thoughts on their business transaction, she tapped on the page. "We'd be interested in a dresser and a chest of drawers, too. Maybe a chair?"

"A rocking chair?" Mia's eyes widened. "And, like, a cedar chest, you know, to put at the end of the bed and sit on?"

Jonah's chuckle was a warm surprise. "I could do that."

He had wonderfully strong hands and thick, scarred fingers that looked like he could do anything—and had. There was something in his shadowed eyes, something in the tense angle of his jaw, the way he kept his feelings carefully controlled that made her wonder more about him. About where he'd been and what he'd done. Why he limped. Why a man who looked strong and capable enough to save the world was making furniture in a carpentry shop in Chestnut Grove.

He's not any of your business, Debra, she reminded herself.

He moved a bit closer, turning the page of his book to show a photograph of a similar bedroom set. She hardly noticed the writing desk that made Mia gasp for the man whose gaze found hers.

In that moment, between the beat of her heart and the next, it felt as if time stretched again. She saw a glimpse of the answers—and of the man—in his expressive gold-flecked eyes. In the raw pain that moved across his handsome face.

Before she could begin to wonder, the outside door snapped open, a gust of frigid air rolled between them and her heart started beating again. The moment was gone, time marched on and Jonah lifted one hand in a welcoming greeting to the newcomer, leaving Debra wondering if she'd imagined the moment.

But before she could think on it any further, Mia was shouting. "Uncle Ben! Mom, it's Uncle Ben!"

And all questions—and curiosity—about Jonah Fraser were put on hold.

Chapter Three

Debra watched Ben close the door against the cascade of snow that had tumbled in with him. Her half brother. She still couldn't get over it.

"Whew," he said, unwrapping the muffler from around his throat. "It's really starting to come down out there. Mia, it's good to see you again. You're looking very Christmassy."

"It's my new sweater. See? It has real bells on it." The girl jumped up and down until the tiny bells sewn into the sweater tinkled cheerfully. "I'm *so* glad you came back!"

"I wouldn't miss you and your mom's visit for the world." Ben had a kind look to him, a down-to-earth quality that it was hard not to like.

And she'd tried, Debra thought. Big-time. She didn't want to like him. She still didn't want to like him, but he had a friendly smile that was hard not to return. A few months ago, he'd come out to Maryland to meet them. While it had gone fairly well, she still wasn't ready to welcome him with open arms. She didn't know him. She didn't know if his claim to the family was a good, positive thing, or if it would turn out to be something they all regretted. You couldn't see a person's true motives in one meeting and a few phone calls.

Sure, call her wary, but she felt that, unlike other members of her family, Ben needed to prove himself a good man before she accepted him. She was determined to keep her defenses up.

"Debra." He nodded once in greeting, glancing over the top of Mia's brown hair. He looked a little stiff, too, and a little wary.

She knew just how he felt. There was no telling where this would go. Meeting one another had been one thing, but to try to establish a relationship? That involved risk; someone—especially Mia—could get hurt.

"I'm glad you made it here safe," Ben was saying. "The roads are tough-going."

"Yes, they often are this time of year." She heard the stilted sounding words come out of her mouth and she couldn't seem to think of anything more friendly to say.

But she *was* strikingly aware of Jonah and

her emotions seemed to warm for him as he snapped the binder shut and turned away with it, walking with that uneven gait that made her care. Why him? And why for him, when she couldn't let herself warm up her frosty feelings toward her half brother? She didn't like this at all. She was accustomed to being very in control of her emotions.

"Sorry I wasn't here to meet you two." Ben hung his coat up on a rack by the door. "Thank you for waiting for me."

It was Mia who jumped in with an answer. "Like we'd come all this way to *not* wait? So, when do I get to meet my cousin, Olivia? And baby Joseph? Now?"

Ben chuckled, his gaze softening with kindness; it was hard not to like someone who was good with her daughter. "Soon, I promise. They're home with Leah. You know, Olivia can't wait to meet you, too. Debra, Leah is especially excited to meet you both. We were hoping you'd come to the tree-lighting ceremony with us tonight."

Mia jumped in. "What tree lighting? Is it a special ceremony?"

"Yep. It's a town tradition over at the mayor's mansion." Ben's chuckle of amusement at Mia's enthusiasm was nothing but gentle.

Debra could already feel the ties pulling at her like invisible strings of obligation. She'd learned that people were unknown quantities. The last thing she wanted was for Mia to get hurt. To get her hopes up, as she always did, only to be crushed if this didn't work out. The Cavanaugh family might not want real ties; maybe this invitation to town was about getting their curiosity satisfied. Who knew what the future held? Mia's heart could be broken.

To make matters worse, she couldn't seem to concentrate on the conversation. Jonah was re-shelving the binder, moving with that disciplined control of his. A lightbulb went on. He had the posture and manner of an elite soldier, that's what he reminded her of, she realized. Although she couldn't reconcile that with this man who made such beautiful, intricate furniture.

She realized Mia was staring at her again, as if expecting an answer. "Oh, the tree lighting. What time is that happening?"

"At eight o'clock sharp." Ben strode toward her. "It's a big event here. There'll be music and the church choir will be singing carols. Mia, I've heard rumors there might even be a visit from old Saint Nick. There will be bags of candy for the kids, prizes and a church raffle.

It's a good, family-friendly event. We've all been looking forward to it. Leah made reservations for all of us at the Hamilton Hotel's restaurant beforehand."

"It sounds lovely." What else could she say? She knew it was right when Ben grinned. He had a smile that was a little ghost of her mother's—*their* mother's, would she ever get used to that? And it made Debra sad in more ways than she could count.

Her throat felt tight as she said, "I look forward to meeting your wife. Leah sent us the nicest letter just last week. I hope she received my response."

"It came in yesterday's mail."

The contents of Leah's letter had been nothing earthshaking. It was simply a very nice and inviting letter telling more about the extended Cavanaugh family, the town, its history and the best places for them to stay. "We have a room at the Peachtree Bed and Breakfast on her recommendation. It's a cozy inn, just as she promised."

"I'm glad it helped out." His cell phone rang and he pulled it out of his pocket to check the screen. "Oh, speaking of the wife. It's her. Excuse me, won't you?"

"Certainly." Debra stepped away to give

him privacy and Mia danced up to her, lit with excitement.

"I've never been to a real tree lighting before. Uncle Ben knows I don't believe in Santa Claus, right? I mean, that's for little kids."

"It's just for fun, you know that." Debra had grown up in a family where Santa Claus was a secular icon and therefore not part of her childhood, but she didn't feel as strongly on the subject as her mother had. Millie had been a very strict Christian and disciplinarian. Debra smoothed back a lock of Mia's baby-fine hair out of her eyes, glad that so far things were going well.

Then a blur of movement at the edge of her vision caught her attention.

Jonah. He was the reason that she'd been distracted throughout her conversation with Ben. The big man had hunkered down to his work carefully sanding a portion of the crib. Debra couldn't help noticing how his big artist's hands expertly worked the small square of roughened paper over the delicate scroll-work, she supposed to get it exactly right.

She didn't know him, but what she did know about the man she liked very much. He was so disciplined and exacting. He obviously cared about his work. It must take a lot of the patience and dedication to build something so intricate and perfect.

She admired that kind of stick-to-it-ness. The muscle-bound man looked out of his element kneeling in front of the delicate crib. She never would have pictured him as a minister's son.

The man was an interesting contradiction; maybe that's why she kept wondering about him. Why her eyes kept finding him. Why he stayed at the edges of her mind. He seemed different from most men she knew. In the corporate world, she dealt with a lot of power-hungry men, men concerned with their image, wearing the right suit, driving the right car and having the right title beneath the name on their business cards.

Men like that, she deeply suspected, were like Mia's father. Men who made promises they couldn't keep, weren't man enough to keep.

Jonah looked like a man who knew how to keep his promises and honor his commitments. Not that she was seriously considering even trying to date again. No, it wouldn't be good for Mia to get attached to a man who decided, in the end, to leave.

Debra pushed that old sadness out of her heart and smoothed the last of the damp remains of snowflakes from her daughter's hair.

"Mom," Mia leaned in to whisper. "Isn't Uncle Ben the greatest?"

"He sure seems to be." Please let him be, she wished. Not that she was religious anymore, but if she were to pray, she would have one simple request. *Please, let this work out. Don't let Mia get hurt.*

"Mom. We get to go to the dinner at the hotel tonight, too, right?"

"Of course, kid. If it's what you want."

"Uh, ye-ah!" Mia grabbed Debra's hand and held on tight, the way she used to do when she was a little girl. There was so much brightness in her smile and so much hope in her spirit that it just shone right out of her. "Isn't this the greatest day ever?"

"Well, it certainly has been a very good one."

"Uh-huh! Remember how we never thought we'd get over being so sad when Grandmother Millie died? I've been praying and praying ever since. And look what happened. God found us more family to love."

Mia's hopes were far too high. They had both taken her mother's death hard, each in her own way. Mia was only now just starting to come out of the grief.

Debra felt a horrible sinking feeling in her chest. What could she do to protect her daughter? She didn't have a single idea. Not that she believed a prayer made much difference, but if it could, she hoped hers had risen on angel's wings. What were the chances of all this with Ben coming out all right?

They had talked about that on the drive here to Virginia. Debra had done her best to try to be sensible and prepare Mia for the truth of relationships. You just couldn't know how people were going to decide to treat you.

There was Jonah, watching her out of the corner of his eye. Or was that her imagination?

When she turned toward him, he was absorbed in his work. Acting as if he didn't know she was on the same planet, much less in the same room.

Fine, it was her imagination, after all.

"Leah says hi and welcome," Ben said as he pocketed his phone. "You *are* coming to our precelebration dinner, right?"

"Right!" Mia jumped in with a high-pitched answer. "Cousin Olivia's coming, too, right? And baby Joseph?"

Ben's chuckle of delight was charming. "Absolutely. Olivia's talked about nothing else for days. And talked and talked. Girls," he said, shaking his head in friendly amusement. "If it wasn't for baby Joseph, I'd be really outnumbered."

"You don't look like you're suffering much," Debra commented, unable to keep from sharing a smile with her half brother.

"No complaint here. I've got more blessings than I can count. Family, that's what's important." He shot a look over to the workman crouching strategically behind the crib. "I keep telling Jonah that, but to no avail. He's still stubbornly single. I keep hoping to change that."

"He doesn't even have a girlfriend?" Mia perked up at that bit of news, twisting toward the woodworker to study him intently. "Is that true, Jonah?"

"Yep, it's true." He grinned over the top of the crib. "I'm too busy to have a girlfriend. I keep telling your uncle Ben that, but does it look like he listens?"

"No." Mia answered. "How can you be too busy to have a girlfriend?"

"Look at me, working through lunch. Next thing I know, I'm working away and I look up and it's way past dinnertime."

"That's just like my mom." Mia wrinkled her nose. "She's always at the office. And when she isn't, do you know where she is?"

Debra could feel Jonah's gaze on her. And Ben's, too. She felt her chin shoot up and all her defenses, too. It wasn't easy being a single parent, but she was doing her absolute best.

The big man on bended knee reached for a fresh sheet of sandpaper. "If your mom's anything like me, she probably brings work home."

"That's it exactly," Mia confirmed.

"I don't think it's much of a secret why she works so hard."

"It isn't?" Mia took a step toward him, transfixed.

Deb realized that's how she felt, too.

"Nope, it's easy to see." Jonah's baritone sliced right through her every defense. "She works that hard for you. Isn't that right, Debra?"

"Y-yeah." With her shields down, she felt the impact of his words with her unprotected heart. She'd walked around with those shields up for so long, she felt way too exposed. The odd thing was, she also felt touched that this man she'd only just met understood her. "That's right, Jonah."

Their gazes met. No one had ever seen her truth so clearly.

"Seems that we have a lot in common, Debra." Ben, who'd been quietly watching them, stepped forward, into the light. "We're more alike than either one of us guessed."

Her throat ached with emotion. "Maybe we are."

"So, Jonah." Mia, irrepressible Mia, focused her big innocent eyes on the woodworker. Again. "Don't you want a family?"

Here we go again. Deb mentally groaned. What was she going to do about her child? The girl cared about everyone. That wasn't a bad thing in itself, of course, but all anyone had to do was to look at poor Jonah, blushing a bit as he debated exactly how to answer, to see that he needed rescuing. "What was I just saying to you, kiddo?"

"Oh, that I'm not supposed to, uh, pry?" She shrugged a lock of silken curls behind her shoulder. "Oh, yeah, I forgot. Sorry, Jonah. Can you forgive me for prying?"

"Sure I can, little lady." Jonah gave a wink, maybe to show there were no hard feelings.

He was a patient man and kind to her daughter. Debra couldn't help seeing more to like in him. "Maybe it's time to drag you out of here."

"Mo-om." Mia gave an impatient but indulgent sigh, as if to say it was hard raising a parent. "Uncle Ben just got here and everything, and besides, I still want to know about Jonah. So, can I pry just a little more?"

Debra bit her lip to keep from smiling and noticed both men in the background trying to do the same. And failing. Some days it was truly hard not to chuckle 24-7 when Mia was around. "She's so like our mother, Ben. I know you have to be wondering about Mom. Well, she and Mia were so alike. Hardly different at all."

Ben's eyes silvered even as his smile broadened. Their mother's smile. There it was again. "Then I know I would have loved her."

Debra swallowed hard, determined to keep her emotions well controlled, just as emotions ought to be. "Mia, instead of peppering Jonah with personal questions, you might want to be gathering up all your favorite stories about Grandmother Millie to tell your uncle Ben this evening at dinner."

"That'll take a long time. I've got *a lot* of stories."

Ben cleared his throat. "I'll look forward to hearing them."

Which was just the opportunity she was looking for—a chance to leave. Debra's chest felt tight. So many painful emotions were beating right along with her heart and she still felt vulnerable. Her defenses were down. Way down. This wasn't how she was used to feeling.

She took a step backward. "Mia and I will meet you at the hotel's dining room, then, and we'll bring our best stories of Mom with us."

"I'd like that." Ben swallowed hard, emotions playing on his face.

This had to be hard for him, too, she realized. That she'd never considered his end of things before surprised her now. It just went to show how off-center she'd been, how jumbled up, wrestling with grief over their mom's loss and so many past issues being dug up. Ben seemed like a strong, assured man, but maybe he had the same worries. How would this work out in the long run? Would they find a way to bond? Or would, in the end, this attempt to get to know one another not work out?

Ben had taken the first risky steps. Maybe she could make one, too. "I'm so glad you invited us to visit. I look forward to getting to know my older brother better."

He dipped his chin in thanks and his throat worked. He said nothing, but Debra knew she'd done the right thing. While she didn't know how this would all turn out, she suddenly wanted it to work out, not just for Mia, but for herself. Mia was right. They'd lost Mom and now it seemed they were being given a chance for more family to love.

Would this help to heal the pain in her own life? Debra had to wonder. Either way, she had to make sure she did her part in all this, for Mia's sake. She could see beyond the girl's excitement and hope right down to the pain she carried inside. The pain of her grandmother's loss. Maybe this would help heal that, too.

"Tonight, then." Debra nodded to her brother, taking another step back, and there was Jonah, once again, within her sight. "You'll let me know about the furniture? I imagine you'll need a deposit or you'll have an invoice or something to that effect?"

"Ben has your number. I'll have him get ahold of you." The carpenter looked up from his work, frozen in motion. "I'll write up an invoice so you'll know the cost of things. I'll draw up some plans, just to make sure Miss Mia gets exactly what she wants. Would you like that, little lady?"

"Oh, yes!"

Debra knew one thing—it was safer to take another step backward and another until she was at the door and far from Jonah. "Come now, Mia. We need to get ready for tonight and I'm sure your uncle and Mr. Fraser want to get back to their work."

"But Mom, I've got the best idea." Mia

clasped her hands together. "Uncle Ben, would it be all right if Jonah came with us tonight?"

Ben gave her a friendly wink. "You don't think I've already tried that? I asked him and he said no."

To Debra's horror, Mia bounded up to Jonah. "You'll come, right? If you do, we'll have the greatest time. Plus, my mom will have someone to talk to. She really needs that."

What? Debra's jaw dropped. *What had her daughter just said?*

If Jonah was uncomfortable before, he looked embarrassed now. A blush swept across his stony face, but his eyes when he answered looked infinitely sad. "Sorry, Mia. I have to say no."

"But my mom—"

"Mia." Debra hoped she sounded unaffected as she held out a hand for her daughter, but that wasn't how she felt at all. Mortified, yes. Embarrassed, absolutely. And surprisingly intrigued. But that wasn't a feeling she wanted to examine too closely. "Don't traumatize poor Mr. Fraser any more. I'm sure he has better things to do than to be forced to talk with me through dinner."

"But Mom—"

"No buts." She smiled when her daughter

clomped closer and took her hand, such a good girl at heart. "We should have time to stop by that bookstore you saw on our way back to the Inn."

"Okay." Mia didn't look satisfied, but she apparently was willing to retreat a little bit for the moment. "'Bye, Uncle Ben and Jonah. See you later!"

The men called out their goodbyes and Debra gave them one last look before she headed outdoors. The chill of the December afternoon wrapped around her, but her face, by contrast, felt shockingly hot. As the door snapped shut and Mia hopped cheerfully through the snow to the SUV, Debra caught one last sight of Jonah, head bowed and kneeling before the cradle in that soft gray fall of light, already back to work.

She felt vulnerable, oddly open at heart, and she didn't know why. Debra dug out her keys, resolved to put the man out of her thoughts and followed her daughter through the falling snow.

Inside the warm building kneeling before the crib, Jonah kept his head bowed over his work. But was he paying attention to what he was doing? No. He couldn't seem to keep his gaze from the sight of Debra Cunningham Watson sweeping the mantle of snow off the windshield of her fancy vehicle.

"What do you think of that?" Ben asked with a smile in his voice.

Jonah didn't look at him, but swung his attention back to his work. Ben didn't sound as anxious as he had earlier. No, he sounded almost…amused. "Looks like you've got a real nice sister and niece."

"I think so, too." Ben gave a chuckle as he nodded toward the window. "Maybe you should come along tonight. I might need some help."

So that's what this was about. Jonah set down the square of sandpaper and straightened up. "Ben, don't. You already know my answer."

"True, but you can't blame me for trying again. I know you, Jonah. Before you went off to right the world's wrongs, you always used to talk about wanting a wife one day. A family."

Jonah grimaced inside, remembering how idealistic he'd once been. "I was just out of boot. What did I know? I was young then."

"Well. You went off, saved the world just like you wanted to. Now it's time to work on those other dreams."

"Not so easy, bud." Jonah tried to act like it was no big deal, but his friend's words made him bleed from a wound so deep, there was no measure of it. Ben had no idea what he'd said. Jonah cleared his throat, determined to make the best of it. After all, he had nothing to complain about, not really. Not when he was alive and well unlike— He stopped that thought. "These days, I'm a busy man and getting busier by the minute. I just got a huge order from that classy sister of yours. I'm making a bedroom set for your niece."

"So that's what all that invoice talk was about."

"You think I'm interested in her?"

"It's the Christmas season." Ben seemed to dodge the question. "You never miss the tree lighting so you'll be there anyway. You might as well come along with us tonight. Make an evening of it."

"That's your family time. I won't intrude on that."

"You're practically part of the family." Ben gestured to the window. "Besides, I'm not the only one who would like you to come along."

There was Mia, sitting in the passenger seat, her hands clasped tightly together. Their gazes met and her eyes widened. There was no mistaking the single word she was saying. "Please, please, please, please."

Ben chuckled. "I think she's serious."

"Sure looks like it." Okay, so he was a little tempted to change his mind.

"You and Debra seemed to get along pretty well," Ben said.

Debra. She wasn't watching him as she backed her top-of-the-line SUV out of the parking spot. Hard to tell exactly what she thought of him, but he knew one thing. She was out of his league. Which was too bad. He liked her—then a powerful wave of old guilt crashed through him. He had no right to take that thought any further.

"Well, buddy, at least think about coming with us. Olivia will be disappointed, too. You don't want to let down two little girls now, do you?"

"When you put it like that, you know I can't."

"I know." Ben grinned and because his business cell phone chose that moment to ring, he answered it.

Debra's SUV pulled into traffic and out of his sight, but the woman seemed to linger in his thoughts. Grimly, he went back to work, ignoring the sting of an emotion he would not admit or give name to.

Chapter Four

"I'm sorry you didn't have a better time at dinner," Debra said, tongue in cheek, to Mia as they drove through the nighttime residential streets of Chestnut Grove.

"I know!" If she hadn't been held secure by the seat belt, Mia would have bounced out of the seat with happiness. "Aren't you glad we came? I sure am! Dinner with our new family was great and it was so fun. Oh, look at that. It's so cute!"

And so it went as Debra tried to keep Ben and Leah's minivan in sight. The falling snow made it difficult and the streets as they approached the mayor's mansion were increasingly busy. Debra halted at a crosswalk for a family of four to cross safely and lost sight of the van completely. While they waited for the happy-looking family to cross, Mia went on about the decorated houses and light displays and how Christmassy it was in this small town. That was, of course, when she wasn't going on about the new members of their family.

Another family stepped into the crosswalk and she waited, the windshield wipers swiping on high speed at the furiously falling snow. Mia's singsong voice, bright with joy, did add to this special evening. Her daughter was happy. That was all that mattered.

When there was both a break in the pedestrian traffic and a pause in her daughter's monologue, Debra managed to get a word in. "The directions Leah gave me are in the glove compartment. Could you get them out please?"

"Sure. Didn't we have the best time? I just love my new cousins. I knew I would! Baby Joseph is so sweet! They have a dog named Bear. I want to get a dog one day. And can you believe Olivia is a singer? She loves singing in the choir, too!"

"You were like two peas in a pod at dinner."

"Can you believe it? I just love her. And Aunt Leah is so nice and pretty. Don't you just love her, too?"

"It's hard not to." That was only the truth. She couldn't remember the last time she'd had such a pleasant meal with kinder people. Ben's wife, Leah, was even nicer in person than she'd been in her letter and on the phone. Before the appetizers had been served, Debra had already felt comfortable with her new sister-in-law. And Ben and Leah's children were as delightful as could be.

Nine-year-old Olivia and Mia had been instantly taken with one another and, although a few years separated them, they'd talked on and on about their new boots, which were a match, their schools, Olivia's dog and the books they liked to read. They both loved music and singing and church. Ben and Leah's baby, Joseph, was obviously well-loved and adorable with a wide baby grin and fine, fuzzy light brown hair.

"Here's the directions!" Mia handed over the note from Leah and strained against her seat belt, trying to see all the decorated homes that lined the way. "Mom! Look! There's an entire street all done up in lights. It's perfect!"

Debra didn't dare take her eyes from the road, so she couldn't look to where her daughter was pointing. She held the directions against the steering wheel so she could watch the weather, the traffic, the pedestrians who were crowding along the sidewalks and crosswalks and follow Leah's step-by-step instructions all at the same time.

"Oh, I want to drive down that way and see the street of lights. Can we? Please?"

"We can't, not now. We'll miss the ceremony that you *so-oo* wanted to see." Debra imitated Mia's cool, teenagery tone and they both laughed.

"I meant later, not now." Mia rolled her eyes, but the wide smile remained on her sweet face.

Seeing her daughter so happy felt like an answered prayer. Did she dare hope that the worst of their recent conflicts was over? Debra spotted a space along the curb and hoped they'd be able to squeeze into it. She turned on her blinker and began to back into the spot.

"Mom! Mom! I can see the mayor's mansion! See all those lights?"

"Not at the moment." Amused, Debra straightened out the wheel and watched the mirrors carefully as the SUV came to a stop against the curb.

"But I can see our new family, too." So much excitement. Mia escaped from her seat belt. "See? Don't they look like a Christmas card with the way they are right in front of the lights?"

Debra gave the wheel a final turn, the front tire nudged the curb and she turned off the engine. As she squinted through the snow-flecked windshield, she didn't notice the blaze of decorations that had Mia so enraptured.

No, her gaze went straight to the perfect family. The crowd, the storm and her worries faded as she watched her older brother—she still wasn't used to saying that—with his family. He held his wife's hand and as the two gazed at one another, the tender look and loving smile they shared was unmistakable. Theirs was a deeply loving and close marriage. Even from across the street and through the haze of snowfall, Debra could recognize that.

If she had any worries left about the kind of man Ben was, they melted like the snow on the windshield. He was the kind of man his family could trust. The kind of husband his wife could not only depend on, but turn to, always. Earlier, through their dinner at the hotel, Leah's opinion of her husband was hard to miss. The trusting way she turned to him, the secret smiles they shared, the adoring way she watched him when he wasn't looking—it wasn't superficial. Even someone as jaded as she could see that Ben was a wonderful husband and father. One of the good ones.

Proof that there were a few good ones in the world.

"Mom!" Mia tumbled out of the SUV. "Look! There's Jonah!"

Talk about another good one. Not that she was noticing. And to prove it to herself, she kept her eyes down, turned away, gathered her purse and her gloves and opened the door. The cold night air took her breath away. It couldn't be the big, stoic man striding toward her with the crunch of ice beneath his boots. She closed the door and realized she'd left her keys in the ignition.

Way to go, Debra. Way to act unaffected. She grabbed the keys, aware of the man's presence like the gravity on her feet. She was as aware, too, of the rumble of his baritone over the beat of her own heart. She closed the door, locked up and zipped the keys into the outside pocket on her handbag.

"Jonah, you came!" Mia clasped her hands together in pure delight. "Thank you, thank you, thank you! I knew you would. But you should have had dinner with us. I had a choco- late-cookie cheesecake and it was the best ever!"

"I'm sorry I missed it."

"Plus, then you could have talked with my mom."

Jonah chuckled in that easy way of his. "I'm

sure your lovely mother had plenty of people to talk to at the table, especially if you were there."

Debra bit her lip, trying to keep from smiling, but it didn't work. She pulled on her gloves and joined her daughter and the amicable Mr. Fraser on the sidewalk, trying to ignore the wash of peace she felt simply from being near to him.

Mia rolled her eyes, lighthearted. "Okay, okay, so I talk just a little too much."

"Just a little?" Jonah gently teased.

Mia only seemed more delighted. "I know, sure, I talk too much. But I just have so much bubbling up from my spirit. My grandmother Millie used to say I'm like the sun shining, except I don't shine, I talk."

"Hey, I wasn't complaining. Your grandmother must have been a very fine lady. You both must miss her a lot."

Mia added sweetly and sadly all at once. "We really do."

Debra watched, riveted by this man. "Mom would have loved being here, meeting her son, his family and his friends. She would have loved this town."

"There's a lot to love about it." Jonah didn't meet her gaze as they walked along. "It's the reason I always come back."

"You've lived in other places?" she found herself asking. Hadn't she decided not to ask questions about this man?

"I've been around. I joined the marines for a few hitches. The greater good and all that." His voice sounded light and dark all at once, but if that made him sad, he didn't let it show. "But the old adage is true. There's no place like home."

The marines. It didn't come as a big surprise. His being like a soldier had been her first impression of him. She wouldn't have been surprised if he'd said he was Special Forces. He kept to the outside edge of the sidewalk protectively and it was an old-fashioned thing to do, gentlemanly.

Wasn't she going to stop noticing all of Jonah's fine attributes? She wasn't the kind of woman who looked twice at men. And yet her gaze kept finding him in the half-shadows.

Mia chimed in. "That's what I keep telling my mom. The Stanton School is not home and I don't want it to be."

Here we go again. Debra wasn't sure what to do with her daughter's stubborn streak. Once she decided something, she was like a speeding train on a track. "It's a big adjustment to get used to living away from home. You have to give it time, Mia."

"Wait one minute. Why the new bedroom set?" Jonah sounded surprised. "I thought you'd be using it."

"Only when I'm home for a school break." Mia sighed, greatly burdened, but beneath the bit of dramatics, there lurked an honest note of sorrow. "Mom and me are hardly together at all because I'm away from home. And now that Grandmother Millie's gone, it's like I'm a-loone."

She'd never heard Mia say it quite that way before, and it made her heart ache. "I get lonely for you, too, kid."

"I know." Mia didn't seem to doubt that. "I'm all miserable and stuff, but, hey, I gotta go because it's *tradition* and it's sooo important."

Why hadn't she ever heard the pain beneath her daughter's sarcasm before this? It was Jonah. It was as if her inner defenses went down when he was near. With the shields around her heart nonoperational, she felt her daughter's loneliness as sorely as her own. "We'll talk about this later, Mia. This isn't the time."

"But—"

"Tradition *is* important." Jonah spoke up. "I bet that's an awful nice school you get to go to. Not everyone gets an educational opportunity like that."

"I guess." Mia was polite about it, but she

clearly didn't agree. "I just don't like going away to school."

"There are worse things in this world."

Although he'd said the words simply, why did she feel the weight of his grief in them? It was Jonah. Being near to him made her vulnerable and oddly open at heart.

To make matters worse, Debra couldn't help admiring the way Jonah was the first to step into the sidewalk, protectively checking traffic before she and Mia followed a half a step behind. It was a small thing, but a nice thing to do and it just went to show what a gentleman Jonah Fraser truly was.

Wasn't she going to stop noticing all of Jonah's fine attributes? It only proved how overworked and overstressed she was. She breathed in the fresh crisp air, felt the caress of snow against her face and smiled at the family who had stepped out of line to greet them.

Debra wished she'd worn earmuffs when Mia and Olivia ran toward each other with a few shrieks and giggles and joined hands, talking excitedly.

"I'm so glad for the girls." Leah, with the baby cradled against her, smiled in that kind, lovely way of hers. "Look at the two of them. They're like long-lost friends."

"It's wonderful," Debra agreed, aware of Jonah as he and Ben exchanged pleasantries. "It's just what Mia needed."

"Olivia, too. I hope you and Mia can spend a lot more time with us before you have to head home." Leah paused as the infant stirred. "I was hoping you might want to spend tomorrow afternoon with us. Maybe stay for dinner?"

"We would love to." Debra truly meant that. She heard Jonah's low rolling chuckle, and it was a warm cozy sound that seemed to chase the chill out of the wintry night. Since she wasn't noticing Jonah Fraser at all, in the slightest, Debra kept her back turned to him and leaned to get a glimpse of the baby as he stretched and yawned. "He's adorable. You are so lucky."

"I'm greatly blessed and I know it." Leah's contented sigh said everything. "Two years ago I was alone and now look. I have my daughter back and my wonderful Ben. Joseph came along to add even more happiness. Now I have a new sister and niece and the rest of your family we have yet to meet. God is gracious, indeed."

"That's what my mother would always say."

"I know I would have liked her."

"She would have liked you right back." Time

was making the sorrow easier, but now and then it came fresh in waves. So many emotions tugged at her from different directions. The issues with Mia. Her unusual reaction to Jonah. Ben, and all the lies her mother had told her. And now this, seeing her little nephew, so sweet and dear, and wanting— Oh, everything she could not have. "You need to come to Baltimore and meet everyone there. I was hoping you could come stay for New Year's."

"I'd like that. I'd have to talk it over with Ben."

"I understand. I have a big house with room for everyone. You would be welcome to stay. We don't do much for New Year's Eve, but we always have a feast on the first. We would love to have you come visit."

The baby chose that moment to let out a whimper. Leah snuggled him and, pleased with the attention, he blew a bubble and grinned. Ben settled his hand on Leah's shoulder and gazed down at their son. "Want me to take over?"

"I think he's missing his daddy."

"Good thing. I was missing him, too." As Ben lifted his son from his wife's arms, Olivia skipped up to him with Mia at her side.

"Dad, they're giving out *huge* bags of candy this year. Did you see them? Can we hurry, please?"

"Sure thing, peanut," Ben said tenderly.

There was no mistaking Ben's deep love for his wife as their gazes locked. Dusted with snow and the glow from the Christmas lights, they looked picture perfect. He took Leah's hand in his and they headed off together.

Clearly, her big brother and his wife had something beyond a good match. True love.

Good for them.

Debra's heart sighed, just a little. She wished real love was a little easier to find. So far, true love had been elusive for her. Deep down, she was afraid she would never find it. Deep down, she was afraid to admit she had never given up hope that she might.

Footsteps crunched in the snow behind her. Jonah. "They make it look easy, don't they?"

She tried to hide her wistfulness, but she could hear it in her voice. "Yes, they do."

Jonah lifted his gaze to hers, and the background murmur of conversations and falling snow faded into nothing. For one brief moment, there was only Jonah. Only his smile, his nearness. Only the wish in his dark eyes.

Sweet, innocent longing trickled to life within her. She could not stop it. She could not will it away. She tore her gaze from his but it remained, another vulnerability in her heart.

She walked with Jonah, following the others. What a lovely night. At Jonah's side, Debra seemed to notice everything she'd always been too busy to see. The resonating melody and harmony of a group of carolers. The scent of wood smoke in the winter evening. The whisper of the snow falling everywhere, as abundant as grace.

Yes, it was a beautiful night.

The ballroom was far too fancy for Jonah's comfort, but as a carpenter and a woodworker, he admired the workmanship of the inlaid marble floor, the handworked cherry moldings and the coved ceiling. Children and families milled about. There were refreshment tables set up with plates of cookies and cups of hot chocolate. He knew practically every person in the room—it looked like most of his father's congregation had come, but did he notice a single familiar face?

No. All he could see was the lovely Debra Watson at his side.

"What a nice tradition this is," she said to him in her cool, gentle alto. "Handmade ornaments?"

"What, you don't think they go with the Italian marble?"

"Absolutely. Are they made by the town's children?"

Enchanting. As sweet as a storybook heroine. That's how she looked with the snow melting into diamond glitters in her soft sleek fall of hair. Jonah cleared his throat, trying to keep his poor befuddled mind on their conversation. "The local kids made the ornaments. It's a tradition."

"I'm hearing that word a lot lately." She swept at the mantle of snow melting on her fashionable coat as if shy.

Or uncomfortable. He wondered what a classy lady like her might think of a regular guy like him. "I could mosey along if you have people to see. Or I could… stay."

That was a tough word to get out. He swallowed hard, but that didn't stop his pulse from stalling completely. He hadn't realized until that moment how much he'd wanted to see her tonight.

"Stay."

Her single word made him smile inside. "Sure. You don't like being alone in a strange crowd, is that it?"

"Something like that." Kindness warmed her up and for a moment her proper, polite demeanor slipped away. She looked so young to have ac-

complished so much—young and good-hearted.
She folded a chestnut lock of hair behind her ear,
somehow a self-conscious gesture. "Mia has
abandoned me for her cousin."

"You sound pretty happy about that."

"Ecstatic. It's good to see her so happy." Like
a cloud before the sun, Debra's warmth faded.
She bit her bottom lip, worrying it. "We've had
such a rough time between the two of us lately."

"How long has your mother been gone?"

"A few years. Recent enough that it still
hurts. I was finally truly starting to deal with her
loss and realizing that we'd never be able to
resolve the rift between us. Then Ben came
along and the past is hurting all over again."

He could see it wasn't petty emotion or
blame that made the woman at his side seem
so sad. "I'm sorry for that. You and Mia seem
so tight, I'm surprised you didn't have the same
relationship with your mother."

"It's what I wanted, but Mom was strict. A
tough disciplinarian. She had so many wonderful qualities, but I was the oldest and I got the
brunt of her discipline. Every little thing had to
be right. I loved her. I wanted to please her so
much." Debra winced, as if she were trying to
hold back those painful memories. She turned to
keep her eye on Mia, standing in line with her

cousin in front of the unlit Christmas tree. "I didn't want my baby to grow up the way I did. It's tough enough for Mia to follow in the family's footsteps. The Cunninghams and Watsons have a lot of expectations for their off-spring."

"You're talking about that fancy school she goes to?"

A single nod. "I know how hard it is for her. It's what I had to do, too. It's painful trying to wedge yourself into a mold that will never quite fit. But it's not only family tradition, but also what my mom wanted." She folded her arms in front of her chest, as if shielding her heart. "Thank you for what you said before, about how having an education like that is a privilege. She's so gifted. I'd even go as far to say she's blessed. Mia is exceptionally bright. She's reading at a college level and has been for years. She's the top of her class. She's gifted in music and athletics, too."

"And her personality." Jonah had to agree. "She's like the sun shining."

"Even in winter. You were right about something else, too. She makes everything worth it."

Nothing but pure love in her voice. Jonah's heart skipped a beat at the sound of it. He found

Mia and Olivia in the crowd, side by side, hand in hand, chattering away to one another excitedly. Both lived happy, safe and comfortable lives with opportunity and loving parents watching over them. He squeezed out the memory of some places in the world he'd seen, where children were not so fortunate.

He didn't know if it was his place, because Debra Watson was clearly a good mother and materially successful. He said what he thought anyway. "It's nice to have comforts and the opportunity of a quality education. But don't forget that to Mia, you're a blessing, too."

"Oh, I don't know about that." Debra shrugged one slim shoulder, looking forlorn and uncertain. Tears pooled in her eyes but did not fall. "I hope I'm doing the right thing for her."

"Love is always the right thing. Look how happy she is." Jonah took a step toward the line of children where Ben and Leah were keeping an eye on the girls. "C'mon. Let's join them. I bet I can charm a piece of candy out of Santa Claus, if you want me to."

"Are you friends with Santa, too?"

"You bet. I designed new toy shelves for him when he remodeled."

"Next thing you'll tell me is that you leap tall buildings in a single bound."

"Sorry to disappoint you." Jonah tried not to let her compliment bother him. The wound he carried in his soul ached, the wound that no one in his hometown knew had not healed. He knew it never would, unlike the injury to his leg, which had been very severe. He'd almost lost it. He cleared the emotion from his throat. "I can probably get you a cup of hot chocolate."

"That's music to my ears. A steaming cup of cocoa is my favorite thing."

"Mine, too." How about that? Jonah grinned to himself as he led the way the short distance to the refreshment tables. "I bet you like the fancy upscale kind with flavors like raspberry chocolate."

"Sure, I'm guilty of loving raspberry chocolate, but there's nothing like plain old chocolate with marshmallows. Add a little trickle of chocolate sauce on top and it's heavenly."

"It seems like you and I have a lot in common, I—" Jonah heard someone calling his name, as if from a far distance. He'd been caught up talking with Debra that he hadn't noticed his little sister behind the table, adding whipped cream to the foam cups of cocoa. That couldn't be a good sign.

"Jonah," Dinah gently scolded him, "are you paying attention, brother dear? Who is this?"

Good question. Jonah knew however he answered that question, there was no getting around the fact that he recognized the look of interest on his sister's face. She was going to read something into this that simply wasn't there. Something that could never be.

He cleared his throat again, which ought to have been a sign to him right then and there, and did his best to sound unaffected, indifferent and unyielding. "Debra Watson, I'm sorry you have to meet my younger sister, Dinah."

"Sorry, huh?" Dinah's bright blue eyes lit up with amusement. "Hi, Debra. It's nice to meet you. You're Ben's half sister, right?"

"Right. How lovely to meet you, Dinah." Debra smiled cordially as she accepted a cup of cocoa.

Poor Debra, Jonah thought. He wasn't sure how to protect her from his sister's curiosity— a family trait, or so it was turning out. Everyone in his family kept thinking it was a bad thing he was alone. There was nothing wrong with being a bachelor, but they simply did not agree.

He could see that look on Dinah's face now as she turned her attention on Debra. "Chestnut

Grove is nothing like Baltimore, but it looks as if you're enjoying your stay."

"Yes, my daughter and I are having a wonderful time. She is particularly charmed by the town."

"Daughter? Oh, tell me about her." Dinah immediately topped another cup of hot chocolate with a generous swirl of whipped cream.

"Mia's thirteen. A very interesting challenge."

"Oh, I was a wild child at that age. I know, I'm a minister's daughter, but I guess I had to rebel. I'm over it now." She laughed at herself and offered the second cup. "For your daughter."

"Thanks." Debra took the cup. The diamonds sparkling on Dinah's left ring finger were hard to miss. "That's a lovely engagement ring."

"My Alex is spoiling me already." Dinah radiated happiness. "I'm so excited. We've just set the date."

"Oh, how wonderful. When are you getting married?"

"Next June. Alex is in the Santa Claus line with the kids. Do you see him? In the blue sweatshirt? I'm helping Alex take care of his cousin's children while she is undergoing cancer treatment."

Jonah shuffled close to accept his cup of hot chocolate. "How's she doing?"

"Better than expected. Isn't that wonderful? We have been praying so hard for her." Dinah projected that calm inner peace that seemed to come with deep faith. "Karla is doing so well that it looks like she's coming to visit for Christmas. Isn't that great? It's a real miracle. Her husband, Frank, has been granted leave from the military to come home for the holidays, too, and the kids, Brandon and Chelsea, are so excited."

"Wonderful." Debra swallowed hard and there was no mistaking the pain on her face. "I hope she recovers completely."

"If God's willing." Dinah took an appraising look at her brother.

Uh-oh. Jonah took a step back, but he was afraid it was too late. He loved that his little sis was happy, but she probably was thinking, as Ben did, that there was a particular brand of happiness *he* ought to try—marriage. They didn't understand.

Time to change the direction of his sister's train of thought. "We'd best deliver the hot chocolate. Hand me over another cup, will you? For Olivia."

"Oh, she's such a sweetie. You should hear her sing." Dinah was happy to accommodate his request, mounding whipped cream like a mountain on top of the chocolate. "Debra, you should stay in town long enough to attend the Christmas pageant. We may be a little town, but we know how to do Christmas right."

"I'm beginning to see that."

Before Dinah could ferret out any personal information—he knew her next question would be to figure out if Debra was married or not. Yeah, he knew his sister meant well, but he had to stop her. "I'll see you, later."

"As long as you give me the scoop. I'll look forward to seeing you again, Debra."

Jonah took off and relief washed through him when Dinah didn't call out after them to say something more. Debra looked as if she hadn't minded the inquisition. Her smile was wide, her cheeks were flushed an attractive pink and her eyes were sparkling.

"You're having a good time?" he asked.

"Yes. I'm going to sound a little bit like Mia, but this is such a nice event. I love the carolers."

"They're part of a group from the church." Did he dare admit the truth? "I've been known to sing with them, when I've got the time."

She shook her head once in a dainty show of disbelief. "You?"

"Yep. You probably thought I couldn't carry a tune."

"No." She surprised him with that answer. A

cute little wrinkle eased across her forehead as she narrowed her gaze, as if to get a good look at him. "You have a resonant voice. I'm not surprised at all."

They'd reached the line around the unlighted Christmas tree. The feeling of anticipation rose in the warm air as it was getting closer to the start of the ceremony. Debra made a beeline toward her daughter, who was only a few kids back from Tony Conlon. The owner of the Gift Emporium looked like he was having a ball dressed up as Santa. He had a little boy on his knee, about four years of age. The kid looked familiar.

But who was he? Jonah couldn't place him. Then realization hit. That's right, it was the Matthewses' little boy. Douglas Matthews was the local big-shot TV-host guy. Jonah couldn't say he really knew the man, although he, his wife and son attended church every Sunday.

The wife, Lynda, had her digital camcorder focused on her son, while he whispered in Santa's ear. She was a shy, reserved woman, who kept to herself. There was true love radiating from her as she lowered the recorder and held out her hand to her son. The boy hopped to the ground, clutching his big bag of Christmas candy and politely thanking Santa.

Nice kid. Nice wife. Jonah felt the ache of sorrow for what he could not have. Guilt rolled over him like the crash of noise from the room. Suddenly it was too loud. He was too hot. The crowd crushed around him, although no one had moved closer. Roaring began in his head, the sounds of the night he did not want to remember.

The night he could never let himself forget.

"Hey, Jonah!" He felt a tug on his sleeve. It was Mia, as sweet as spun sugar. The girl was next in line—she'd let Olivia sit on Santa's knee first. She exuded youthful energy, practically bouncing in place. "I know Santa isn't real, but I have the best wish ever. It's what I pray hard for every day. And it's not selfish, either... Well, it's sort of a little for me, but it's mostly for the person I love the most!"

"Your mom?"

Mia bit down on her bottom lip as if to keep the wonderful secret inside. "And it's for other people, too. It's my most secret prayer and I know it's gonna come true."

Debra was in deep conversation with Leah and Ben, holding chubby baby Joseph in her arms. The sight riveted him and it took all his effort to clear the emotion from his throat. He didn't sound normal at all as he nodded toward

Santa. "Give this cup of cocoa to Olivia, would you? Looks like you're up next, Miss Mia."

"Ooh!" The girl took the cup and then hurried to whisper her most secret prayer in Santa's ear.

Jonah's heart stopped beating when Debra looked up to watch her daughter. Unguarded, motherly love transformed her. He could see right into her heart, right into her goodness and see the real Debra Watson. All love and devotion, down to the soul.

A woman like that was far too good for the likes of him.

A loud noise shot out, a clatter above the other noises in the crowded ballroom. Like gunfire, the sound of a car backfiring on the street shot him ruthlessly back into the past, into a full-out flashback. The scent of fresh pine in the air turned gritty and dank. The lull of the caroler's "Silver Bells" faded into the pop-pop of distant gunfire and the bright lights to midnight dark. The flare of rockets shattered the night as they streaked like fireworks over the desert sky. His mind was locked in the past, in Iraq. The cries of help of the wounded civilians caught in the war zone and of his fellow marines rang in his ears. The wind was thick with the coppery scent of blood in the air, on his face, on his hands—

"Good evening, everyone!" the mayor's smooth, politician voice jerked Jonah back into the present.

He swiped the sweat from his forehead. Gulping hard, he swallowed the taste of guilt and death and a past he could not change. He'd gladly give his life if he could, to make right the senseless wrongs of war.

The flashback was over. Had anyone noticed? He looked around. No, all eyes—Debra's especially—were turned toward the podium where the ceremony was in full swing. Weak from the experience, he spotted an empty folding chair against the wall and collapsed into it. Billy, one of the youth group kids, hit the switch. The Christmas tree burst into color and light. The crowd's awe and the children's glee was joyful music that could not drown out his truth.

Jonah fisted his hands. He had no right to that happiness. For a brief moment, he'd forgotten the past. He had started to live, to enjoy himself and to take part in a life he did not deserve. Not when others more deserving hadn't been so fortunate. He thought of the team members he'd let down. His throat turned to sand, the light drained from the world and he was where he belonged, alone, in grief and shadow.

He climbed to his feet. No one would notice if he bugged out now. He'd meant to say hello to his parents, but he hadn't been able to locate them in the crowd. To tell the truth, he'd been too busy thinking of Debra.

Halfway to the door, he felt eyes on his back. He looked over his shoulder. Why wasn't he surprised to see Debra, turned away from the beauty of the Christmas tree, watching with him gentle concern? She arched one slender brow in a silent question.

He did the right thing—the only thing he could do. He managed what he hoped was a grin, held up his hand as a goodbye gesture and walked through the doors and into the cold night. Guilt clawed at him and the frigid wind and icy snow battered him like punishment.

Hours later, when he was in his apartment, dark with shadows, the guilt still had not relented. It remained like a punishment, sharp and renewed.

When he should have been thinking of his failures to his men, he hated that his mind betrayed him. Instead of taking him back to the war in Iraq, his thoughts led him straight to the image of Debra. To the way she'd stood in front of the glistening Christmas tree, so radiant and good, and the soft questioning way she'd looked at him.

Jonah buried his face in his hands and could not find comfort in the cold, dark night.

Chapter Five

The days that passed had been pleasant ones, Debra reflected as she navigated the SUV along the now-familiar path to Ben's carpentry shop. All right, they had been *more* than pleasant, if she were going to be wholly honest with herself.

They had spent fun afternoons with Leah and Olivia and baby Joseph baking Christmas cookies, making Christmas-tree ornaments and luminaries. They'd made dinners in Leah's cozy kitchen and shared family stories over the dinner table. They'd met Ben's adopted brother, Eli, and his wife, Rachel, and their sweet baby, Madeleine. Debra and Leah even had a few outings to themselves, while Ben watched the kids, to buy Christmas presents and poke through the Main Street shops.

So many wonderful memories she'd saved up during the past four days, but what image was the one that seemed to stick in her head more brightly than all the rest? The sight of Jonah walking away from the tree-lighting celebration that first night they'd been in town. She could still see his shoulders straight and strong and yet his head was down, bowed as if by the weight of the world. She'd felt his sadness as surely as if it had been her own.

He didn't only intrigue her; he'd drawn her heart to his. She couldn't say how or why, but the truth was talking with him had come so easily that night. That was something she'd hadn't encountered in a long time. Not on a personal level, anyway.

The question was, why and what was this? Debra tried to keep her thoughts on traffic but the questions just kept coming. Did Jonah feel the same way? Was he interested in her? How could he possibly be interested in a woman with as much baggage as she had?

She could come up with a hundred reasons why she shouldn't allow herself to hope, but it winked to life within her anyway like a string of twinkle lights on a tree.

"Mom? Hello? Mo-oom! Your phone is buzzing. *Again.*"

"Would you check the screen and see who it is?"

"Okay, but if it's your office, it's Friday afternoon. Af-ter-noon." Mia emphasized as she dug a hand into the designer hobo. "You're supposed to be on vacation."

"Yes, but you know me. Work, work, work." Debra smiled because she really didn't mind how hard she worked. But as they cruised past the Christian bookstore, there was something about it that tugged at a long-buried wish. She'd always wanted to own a bookstore from the time she was a little girl. It was the reason why she'd majored in business—so she would be well-equipped to run her own shop. Life hadn't worked out that way.

It did no good to start wishing for what was impossible now. Wishes were for children, she thought. There was no place in her life for them.

So, why did her thoughts linger on the bookstore and then shift to the carpentry shop and Jonah?

Get a grip, Debra, she told herself. This was not like her. To make matters worse, she was going to see him in a few moments and how was she going to handle this strange, budding emotion toward him?

Play it cool, that's how, she thought as she pulled into the carpentry shop's parking lot. She would be sensible, as always. It was best to wait and see.

"It's a text message from Uncle Brandon." Mia bubbled with happiness. "Can I read it?"

"We'll give him a call when we get back to the bed-and-breakfast, how's that?"

"Even better!" Mia slid the cell back into place. "Oh, I can't wait to see Jonah. Don't you think he's nice, Mom?"

Nice? No, that word seemed inadequate for the man, although she wasn't ready to admit that to anyone, not even Mia. "He certainly is nice to make an entire bedroom set for you, and right before Christmas, too."

"That's not what I meant, Mom." She flipped a lock of hair behind her shoulder and gave a look that was both sweet *and* disapproving.

"I know what you meant, kid, and I'm taking the Fifth." Debra pulled into the first available parking spot. Where did her gaze automatically go to? The window where she had first spotted Jonah. He wasn't there, but she sighed deep inside as if something in her heart and in her spirit remembered.

Focus, Debra. You're going to be sensible, right? She cut the engine. "Keep in mind that

Jonah is doing you a favor by fitting your furniture into his schedule."

"He said he had time."

"Yes, but a carpenter as talented as he is has to be in demand. Go easy on him. Try to keep it simple, okay?"

"Mo-*om*." Mia sighed. "I get it. I'm not a little kid, you know."

"Yes, sweetie. I know. Now, zip your coat before you head out—" the passenger door popped open and Mia was already out in the single-digit windchill "—into the cold."

Too late. Mia's door snapped shut and Debra was left alone. Through the icy streaks on the windshield, she saw the reason why Mia had been in such a hurry. The front door was open and there was Jonah, strong and true, looking manly in his long-sleeved shirt and worn jeans.

Debra took her time, gathering her things, making sure she had her keys, bundling up before she stepped out into the elements. And then there was Jonah and suddenly she didn't notice the cold or the sun in her eyes or the ice beneath her boot treads.

"C'mon, Mom!" Mia hopped down the cleared walkway. "Hurry!"

Jonah's rich chuckle warmed the air. "I've heard it said that beauty never hurries."

Was he talking about her? Debra didn't dare read anything into his words—other than the fact that he was good at making compliments. She hitched her purse strap higher on her shoulder as she came closer. "I recognize that line. You read a lot of poetry, do you?"

"I've been known to crack a book or two. Comes from my love of the King James version of the Bible."

"That my favorite, too." She smiled, liking that about him, but he didn't meet her gaze.

Instead, he broke away and held wide the door. "Well, Miss Mia, are you enjoying your stay in here in Chestnut Grove?"

"Totally!" Mia practically skipped into the workshop, her scarf and hood bouncing with her gait. "I love it! Uncle Ben is the coolest. And we've got a whole new family. It's awesome. Right, Mom?"

"Right." Debra passed through the door Jonah held for her and noticed that he didn't look at her.

"That's the way I feel about my sister getting married. It was like being given a big box of blessings." He turned away to close the door after her and shut out the bitter cold.

As she unbuttoned her coat, she realized he was deliberately avoiding her gaze. Disappointment sank like a stone in her heart. She shrugged out of her coat and like the gentleman Jonah was, he was there, helping her out of the garment, which made her like him even more. She couldn't seem to get a thank-you out of her suddenly tight throat.

"Miss Mia, let me get your coat, too." He helped the girl out of her fashionable parka.

With, Debra noticed, the same stoic politeness. He was just being polite, that was all.

"Why don't you two ladies come take a look at what I've sketched up?" Jonah led the way to a big drafting table in the corner, talking over his shoulder, all business. "You've got a few choices for the design, Miss Mia, and if you're not happy, you say the word and I'll draft up something else."

Debra watched her daughter skip over to the table. Mia's hair fell forward as she bent to study the drawings, hiding the reaction on her face. But Debra could read her happiness like a joyful song in the air. She ambled closer to the man and girl, feeling awkward, not knowing what to do.

Mia clasped her hands together. "Oh, Jonah! It's *just* what I wanted."

"You sure? What about the design? I've got other choices, why don't you take a look?"

Jonah moved to raise the wide computer-aided drafted designs to reveal more pages underneath.

"Nope!" Mia, so like her grandmother, always knew exactly what she wanted. "This is perfect. The scrollwork stuff is just right. Mom! You've got to come see. Ooh, I'm so totally excited. I can't wait until it's done. How long will it take to make all this? How long? Could you be done before Christmas?"

Debra mentally rolled her eyes. There went her daughter again, carried away with her enthusiasm. "What did I just finish saying to you, cutie?"

"Oh, right, I know." Mia winced. "I knew that, but I just got carried away. Jonah, thank you so much for working me into your schedule. It doesn't have to be done by Christmas."

Jonah, Debra noticed, didn't look at all troubled. He appeared amused as he stepped back from his drafting table. "Well, one thing is for sure. I'm not Santa, so I don't have a workshop full of elves to help me out."

"Santa's not real, but it's a nice story. My grandmother Millie and I, we used to go shopping for the church toy drive. You know how you can get a bunch of presents that kids want and wrap them up and then they'll be delivered to the family? That's what we did every year. It was sooo much fun. It was sort of like the story of the elves, but I always thought we were honoring the wise men."

"You sound pretty wise to me, Miss Mia." Kind, infinitely kind, Jonah hunkered down to draw out a wooden box from beneath the table.

The fall of light from the overhead windows revealed the box was full of short lengths of woods in different shades of stain with different finish work, but Debra could not stop noticing the man.

"Let's go sit down in the front office with these plans and these samples." Jonah hefted the box. "We'll finalize all our details and snack on the Christmas cookies Leah and Olivia dropped off this morning."

"Are they the ones I helped make yesterday?"

"I wouldn't doubt it."

Debra watched Jonah and Mia amicably talking as if they'd known each other forever. Something stirred in her heart deep beneath the disappointment and the impossibility. She didn't know what the emotion was or why she felt it. She only knew that it was a powerful and pure feeling. Somehow she made her feet carry her forward after the hippity-hop of Mia's gait across the workshop.

As Mia told Jonah of her plans of going to a church activity this evening with her new cousin, Debra did her best not to notice the dependable line of Jonah's shoulders or the uneven pad of his gait. She hung back. He did not look at her as he brought the plate of cookies to the coffee table between a mismatched couch and chair, which sat in a cozy reception area.

"These *are* the cookies Olivia and I made." Mia dropped onto the couch, sinking into the comfortable-looking cushions. "I did all my Christmas trees with white frosting, because they had snow on them. Olivia did hers in green. See?"

"I see." Jonah's kindly grin died when he saw Debra approaching. He nodded once in acknowledgment and went to the hot-water carafe in the corner, where clean cups and boxes of tea bags were perched on a Christmas themed tabletop.

She clutched her purse more tightly, willing her gaze away from the solid line of his back, which he kept firmly turned toward her. See how he wasn't interested in her? Whyever had she thought he was? She mentally shook her head. So, she was intrigued by the man, it was nothing more. It couldn't be. Besides, he clearly didn't feel intrigued by her. Goodness, what was wrong with her?

She skirted the corner of the coffee table to sit down next to Mia. The plans spread out in front of them were amazing. Such detailed and careful work. The hours it must have taken him to do this. When had he found the time?

"Sorry, we're out of hot chocolate." He set a tray on the table beside the cookies. "But we do have a good choice of tea."

"You do. Thank you." Debra felt awkward as she forced herself to lean forward to inspect the boxes of tea he'd slid onto the tray beside three bright red mugs. The hot water sent curls of steam into the air. Debra reached for one of the tea boxes. "There's peppermint, Mia."

Instead of commenting on her favorite herbal tea, Mia paused for a moment and frowned as she did when she was thinking hard. As if coming to some conclusion she came to life and bounced off the couch cushion. "Jonah, you have to sit over here next to my mom. See? I can sit in the chair!"

Debra coughed once in surprise. The box of tea bags tumbled from her fingers and hit the table. What was Mia up to? It was impossible to read anything but excitement in her merry brown eyes. Her face was one big smile as she slipped around the table and dropped into the chair, blocking Jonah from doing so.

Jonah stood frozen with apparent surprise. "Don't you want to sit next to your mom?"

"Nope, I do that all the time." Breezily, Mia grabbed a green-frosted cookie.

Debra felt the shock start to slip away and she could plainly see how uncomfortable Jonah looked as his gaze studied the empty couch cushion beside her—the only other place to sit in the room. He didn't move any closer toward her. Mia was the one always talking about signs, but Debra had to admit *this* was a sign. Poor Jonah.

She decided to come to his rescue. "Mia, come back next to me. We can look at the wood samples together instead of passing them back and forth."

"I don't mind." Jonah spoke up, although it was hard to tell exactly what he was thinking. He bent to grab a white-frosted cookie before he eased onto the corner of the couch—as far away from her as he could physically get.

Yes, that was a definite sign. The trouble was that she couldn't help noticing how fine he looked in spite of his obvious behavior. The slate-gray shirt he wore was exactly the right color to bring out the golden strands in his dark eyes.

Not that she should be noticing that. Of course not. Debra scooted over a tad to give him—and herself—more room.

"Let me know what you like, Miss Mia." Jonah got straight to business by hauling out a length of wood from the box. The girl squinted at it carefully, debating the cherrywood as the carpenter presented her with a sample of red oak.

Debra set a peppermint tea bag in Mia's cup to steep before she did her own. She bit her bottom lip to keep from asking Jonah about why he had ducked out of the tree-lighting ceremony. Why had a former marine chosen to give up fighting for the greater good for being a carpenter?

The answers weren't her business, but that didn't stop her from wondering.

Through the rest of the meeting, she was careful to keep her gaze only on Mia and the wood samples she was very seriously considering. Mia was her heart, her life, her everything.

Debra took a sip of tea, chose a white-frosted cookie and forced every other thought from her heart.

When Mia beamed with happiness at the end of their meeting, Jonah breathed a sigh of relief.

He hadn't realized how tense he'd been, but talking about his work and seeing how happy he'd made the kid already was the gold star at the end of his day. He was grateful to rise from the couch, for his elbow was in dangerously close proximity to the lovely Debra's. Close proximity to her brought out all kinds of feelings—both of longing and regret.

He rubbed the back of his tight neck with the heel of one hand. "Since I have your approval, Miss Mia, I'll get started on your headboard tonight. I'll aim to have the bed finished before you leave. How's that?"

"Stupendous!" The girl clasped her hands together, the perfect image of childhood joy. "Mom, isn't that fab?"

"Sure, it is." Debra had been quiet through their meeting, so when she finally spoke he was aware of every rise and dip of her gentle voice. She gathered the empty cups and set them on the tray. "What did you forget to say to Jonah?"

"I didn't forget, Mom. I'm just too happy to get the words out."

Jonah turned away as Debra spoke with her daughter. He retreated swiftly to the copier with the finalized furniture plans. It had been tough to stay all business, but he had succeeded this far. He wouldn't fail now. Once a marine, always a marine. He didn't know the meaning of the word *quit*.

He only had a few more minutes to keep his feelings under control. He could do it, right?

Right. He set the plans in the copier tray and hit Print. As the copier whirred and clicked and sucked in the original pages, he tried not to listen to the conversation between mom and daughter, but their voices lifted above the drone of the machine.

"C'mon, Mom, you gotta come with us tonight. If you don't come with me, how are you going to be *saved?*"

"Not that again?"

"I promised Grandmother Millie I wouldn't give up until you were."

"Maybe I'm a hopeless case."

"You keep saying it, but I don't believe it for a single minute."

Jonah's gaze flicked to the window and Debra's reflection. She kept a no-nonsense demeanor, but he wasn't fooled. He caught the twinkle of merriment softening the contours of her lovely face, saw the corners of her mouth threatening to turn into a grin.

She was the kind of woman a man would like to go through life with. Jonah punched the power button off, realizing he'd done the one thing he'd promised himself he wouldn't do. He'd crossed the line he'd drawn and now he was no longer thinking of Debra Watson as a customer and his boss's sister.

Way to go, man. He gathered up the copied pages and went in search of an envelope. While he went through the drawers of the desk in the corner and tried not to bump into the Christmas tree nestled up against it, he tried to refocus his thoughts. Business. Customer. Boss's sister.

It wasn't helping. He could hear the soft pad of her boots against the tile, the rustle as she moved to the workshop door and the tinkle of the ceramic mugs telling him that she was carrying the loaded tray from the room to the employee break room, where the sink was.

Mia's skipping gait stopped at the doorway, telling him he wasn't alone. He found an envelope in the bottom drawer and slid the pages into it.

"Here you go." He held them out for her to take. "I'll do my very best job for you."

"Thank you, Jonah. I really mean that. Not just because it's polite, but because you sure are nice. Uncle Ben talks about you all the time."

"No wonder my ears have been burning."

Jonah kept his voice low, because he knew it would carry in the empty workshop and Debra might overhear. "Your uncle Ben is a good guy. We've been friends for a long time, a lot longer than he's been my boss, you know."

"Yeah. That's what he says." She hugged the envelope to her, scrunching her face in serious thought. "Are you coming to church tonight? Olivia's got practice for the Christmas pageant and I get to come watch."

"No, sorry. I've got this very important furniture order to get to work on."

"Mine, right?"

"Yep."

Cute kid. He could see Debra in her. Not just in their similar shades of brown hair and their strikingly cinnamon-brown eyes, but in her innate regal manner. Debra was doing a fine job raising her—apparently alone. That made him wonder about her life. Was she dating anyone?

Not your business, Fraser. He mentally scolded himself to no avail. Apparently he didn't seem able to stop thinking about Debra—and admiring her.

"You aren't gonna do anything but work tonight?" Mia persisted. "Not even to eat? Or anything fun?"

He chuckled. "And why are you so concerned about me, little lady?"

"Because you're so nice and I really appreciate you working me into your schedule. My mom says you're in demand and I should appreciate it. And I do. So, you won't work all the time, right?"

She was a compassionate one, this one. He wanted to reassure her—he worked long hours and into the night often because he could not sleep. Not because he had too much work to do. "I'll work for a bit more this afternoon. Then Ross is coming over to pick up the crib. After that I'll probably mosey over to the bookstore down the way. Pick out a good book to start reading tonight."

"Ah, that sounds good." Mia nodded her approval. "I love to read and my mom does, too. She reads all the time. Do you?"

"I read a lot."

"Good! That's very, very good."

"You'd best run along. Your mom is waiting." He noticed Debra the instant she stepped back into his sight, already wearing her coat and holding Mia's folded neatly over the crook of her arm.

Lovely. She was absolutely lovely and he shouldn't be noticing. This was business, remember? He spun around and held open the door. "You two ladies have a good weekend. Debra, I'll give you a call when I have the bed made and ready for Miss Mia's final inspection."

Debra looked a little puzzled—and distant—as she handed Mia her coat. "That would be fine. I guess this is goodbye for now."

"Yes." He knew it had to be. He didn't figure on seeing her again—other than for business. Sweet longing filled him, but he didn't have the right. Old guilt weighed down his spirit. He stepped aside so the mother and daughter could pass on by. "Goodbye."

That word stuck like sadness in his chest. He thought he hid it well. Debra followed Mia out of the door and into the blinding sunlight reflecting off the snow.

He didn't feel the icy wind or notice the second vehicle parked in the customer lot. Every cell in his brain seemed focused with pinpoint accuracy on the woman who was gently joking with her daughter.

"Jonah. Hey, Jonah." Ross's voice surprised him. He was coming up the walkway. "It's not like you to stare off into space."

"Got things on my mind." Jonah shrugged, unwilling to say exactly what those things might be. He held up a hand to wave, trying to appear casual, as Debra and Mia drove away.

"I think I can see just what things those might be." Ross smiled.

"You didn't hear that from me. That's how rumors get started. Come on in. I've got the crib ready to go. I'll help you load it."

"Sure."

The workshop had always been his escape, but not now. The memory of Debra being here troubled him. He went straight to the crib. "You look like you've been putting in long hours. How's the investigation coming along?"

"Slow. Tedious. Methodical." Ross crouched down on one side of the little cradle. "You wouldn't happen to remember a woman named Wendy Kates?"

"Doesn't ring any bells." Jonah took the other side of the crib. The two men lifted the cradle together. Jonah went through his mind again, sifting the name through his memories. Nothing. "I can ask around if you want. See what I can find."

"I want to keep this hush-hush." Ross grimaced. "The last time I went digging up information on this woman, Kelly's brakes were tampered with."

"I caught you on the news a while back." Jonah backed against the door, paused and hit the bar handle with his elbow. Cold air snaked down the back of his neck as he pushed through the doorway. Ross had made a statement to the local reporters that he'd find the man responsible for Kelly's accident and the damages to the Tiny Blessings Adoption Agency. "You look more determined than you did then."

"I won't let any more harm come to my family. I have to stop whoever is doing this."

Jonah eased his side of the cradle into the back of Ross's vehicle. "You might want to get ahold of my mom. She knows everyone and everything. She's been plugged into this community since she married Dad. She might be able to help you and she knows how to keep a confidence."

"I'd appreciate that." Ross eased his end in and then wrapped an old blanket around the flawless woodwork. "I've hit a dead end. It's as if this woman I'm looking for came out of nowhere. All I can find is her hospital records."

"Take care of your family. You have a precious blessing in them. If you need any help, you know where to find me." Jonah wanted only good things for Ross and his family. "I'm pretty ticked at this guy, too. I'm real fond of Kelly and that baby of yours."

"I know you are. I appreciate it." Ross pulled his keys from his pocket. "I'll give your mom a call. See what she knows. By the way, Kelly is going to love this cradle. Thanks, man."

"Not a problem."

As Jonah watched his friend head off, driving home to a wife and child, he tried not to wish for the same blessings of his own.

Jonah's words followed Ross Van Zandt home. *Take care of your family. You have a precious blessing in them. If you need any help, you know where to find me.*

Protective rage blurred Ross's vision as he pulled into the garage and cut the engine. He had been working long days tracking as many of the pieces of Wendy Kates's life as he could. She was the key to the puzzle.

That poor woman. Ross shook his head as he withdrew the keys from the ignition. He'd found out little information about her since he'd discovered her files among the latest batch of the falsified adoption records found in the Harcourt mansion. He knew that she'd given birth to a baby girl and that trail was cold. He did not know what happened to the infant. Wendy had died during delivery; the cause of death had been blunt-force trauma.

Weeks of work had led him nowhere. The same questions remained. Who was Wendy

Kates? Who was the prominent family member Barnaby Harcourt had been blackmailing to keep quiet about her illegitimate baby? The initials L.M. showed up in the hospital records. That led to more questions. L.M. The name of the man who was being blackmailed? Or the initials of the unnamed father of Wendy's baby?

Whoever that man was, it wasn't a stretch to believe he'd been responsible for Wendy's fatal injury. A man who could kill a pregnant woman— Ross's fists tightened on the steering wheel until his knuckles were white. A man like that was pure evil. He had to be stopped before—

"Ross?" Kelly must have heard him drive up. She cradled a stretching Cameron. They were both safe and happy. That's what mattered. "Ross, you look exhausted. I worry about you. You're working so hard."

"I have to. I've got no other choice." Ross opened the door and kissed his wife tenderly and then his son on his downy head. They were safe for right now, but what if danger struck again? What if he lost them?

On his life, he vowed to protect them.

Chapter Six

The day's end brought tiny crystalline flakes of snow falling from a charcoal sky. Debra hesitated on the cleared walkway outside the adorable little bookshop and took the time to feel the delicate snow brush her face. The cool thrill and fresh scent of it made her feel younger, as if the heavy burden of all her responsibilities could tumble to the ground at her feet, too.

Somehow she felt lighter as she walked toward the little glass door under the blue awning. An overhead bell chimed when she crossed the threshold, welcoming her in.

What a charming place, she thought as she began unbuttoning her coat. It was a small independently owned store. It felt personal and cozy, the way a lot of bookstores used to feel in the days before the larger chains. One of the front bay window displays held a collection of Christmas gift suggestions and books hand-picked by the owner, according to the little calligraphy note card with the special sales price beneath each displayed book. This was all supervised by an orange tiger-striped cat. Sam, according to the tag on his collar, looked as if he were curled up for a nap but opened his eyes just enough to give her an appraising look.

"Hello, there," she said to the cat, itching to brush her fingers across the silken fur. "Do I meet with your approval?"

The cat didn't seem impressed with her and went back to sleep. Debra sighed just a little and moved on, not wanting to disturb the feline. She wished she was at home enough hours in a day to have a fuzzy kitten of her own. Maybe after she had Mia in the college of her choice—okay, her family's choice—there would be time enough to slow down her life. Work less. Have a few little dreams of her own. Maybe a shop like this. A cuddly cat in the window. Time to read the books her company—and other houses—published.

One day, she promised herself, but since she'd been saying that to herself for the last thirteen years, she had a real fear that imagined future just might always be out of her reach. Just a dream, nothing more.

"Can I help you?"

Lost in thought, Debra whirled around to see a smiling, matronly lady at the front counter. She wore dark rimmed glasses. Her silver hair was pulled back in a black hair band. A gold name tag on her red angora sweater said Pamela. When she smiled, she could have been Mrs. Claus.

Debra liked her on sight. "Yes, I need to be pointed in the right direction. I'm looking for your devotional section."

"Straight back, dear. Here, let me show you." Pamela skirted the corner of the counter. "I haven't seen you in my shop before. Are you here in town visiting family?"

"I am." It felt good to say that, for Ben and his family felt as if they were already part of hers. "It must be wonderful to own a little shop like this."

"Wonderful, yes. It's been one of the joys of my life." There was no mistaking the honest affection in her voice. "My Albert and I ran this place together. That is, before his health problems."

Debra remembered how hard it had been to see her mother in pain and so very ill. "I'm sorry to hear that."

"He's past the worst of it, thank the Lord. God has been very gracious, sparing my Albert so we can be together." Pamela halted between the chin-high rows of books near the back of the store and held her hand out toward the rows of devotionals on tidy shelves. "Here are the devotionals, dear. Let me know if I can help you chose one. I've got plenty of suggestions if you need them."

"I'll be fine, thank you. My daughter gave me a few titles to search for." Debra swallowed against the tightness in her throat. "I'm glad your husband is improving."

"He's a testimony to the power of prayer." A tear pooled in the woman's eyes and she swiped it away. "Pardon me. Goodness, life can test your mettle at times. Give me a holler if you need anything."

"I will."

Debra watched the sweet woman go. Pamela had the work life of Debra's dreams. The older lady took her time strolling down the rows, stopping to straighten a book on a shelf here or to swipe a bit of lint off the top of the glossy bookshelves there, or ask another customer if they needed any help.

Life had been so busy for her for so long that she'd forgotten that hardship came to everyone.

There had been no mistaking the love the shop owner had for her husband and for her life here in this lovely little shop, working beside him. A place like this couldn't turn much of a profit, but then, maybe profit ratios and projected returns held little meaning when it came to having a dream.

She felt that dream now, the one so long buried for a life like this one. She loved the way quiet instrumental Christmas music played from the overhead speakers and how the scent of coffee and tea and baked goods drifted from the little café in the corner. She breathed in the smell of new books—one of the best scents in the world, in her opinion. Her eyes smarted. Longing filled her heart with such sore wanting, she felt ashamed. She was a grown woman, in her thirties, a mother of a teenage girl, a vice president of a prestigious and respected publishing house and dutiful daughter to both the Cunningham and Watson branches of her family. As her mother had said so long ago, she should not settle for so little.

As she watched Pamela move about the little store, content and smiling, this did not seem like so little, but like very much, indeed.

A testimony to the power of prayer. Pamela's words stuck with her as she found the title Mia had asked for and wandered through the store. Debra had heard that phrase so much lately, it was starting to infiltrate her thoughts. *The power of prayer.* She'd dismissed such wishful thinking long ago, when she'd been so bleak and alone and when her prayers went unanswered.

Her wavering faith wasn't a result of bitterness or anger at God; it was more like hitting a dead end in a road. There was a big yellow sign and guardrail blocking her way and she could not turn left or right. That's what her faith had come to. There seemed to be nowhere to go with it.

But it hadn't always been that way. As she stopped at the children's section to browse for Christmas gifts for Olivia and Joseph, she remembered when she'd been younger. That was when her life had been sweet and safe and sheltered. She'd had faith, then, and she believed in prayer and a loving God watching over her.

Once she'd had many secret dreams alive in her heart.

Those pesky tears were in her eyes again at the yearning for the chance to turn back time, to go back to that place in her life and hold more tightly to the girl she'd been. To the young woman who believed in the things that could not be seen, only felt.

Was that part of her gone forever?

She didn't know, but she thought she caught a glimpse of that hopeful Debra buried deep inside as she lingered in the aisles full of books so lovingly shelved.

Since she had actual time on her hands, she chose a book for herself on the way to the coffee bar at the other side of the shop. She was in no hurry to head back to the inn and room service.

"Hi," said a teenaged girl from behind the spotless counter. "What can I get you?"

She glanced at the reader board high on the wall behind the teenager. "A large hot chocolate, please. Can I have whipped cream with that?"

"Sure." The kid got right to work.

Debra set the pile of books down on the counter and unzipped her purse. She fingered through the bills in her wallet, looking for a five.

"I'll get that, pretty lady." A familiar baritone rumbled behind her.

Jonah. She looked up and there he was, looking cool—as Mia would say—with his coat unbuttoned and speckled with snowfall. "This is a coincidence. I didn't expect to see you again so soon."

"Imagine that." He tugged his wallet from his

jeans back pocket and strolled closer. "Gina, make that two hot chocolates."

"Sure thing, Jonah," the girl said, her dark ponytail bouncing as she nodded.

Debra pulled out a fold of dollar bills and slid them into the tip cup. "Mia begged me to stop and pick up a new devotional for her. She pleaded. It was the most important thing ever."

"That's why you're here?"

"Yes. What about you?"

He looked contemplative as he dropped a ten on the counter in exchange for the two large whipped-cream-topped cups. "I have a secret bookstore habit."

"Shocking." She followed him away from the counter. "I have a serious bookstore habit, too, when I have the time for it."

He glanced over his shoulder at her, amusement twitching in the corners of his mouth. For a moment it looked as if he were judging his chance of keeping his distance, and then he shrugged. "Something else we have in common. What books have you got there?"

"Nothing interesting." She hugged the stack of books to her to hide the one title she didn't want him to see, as they headed to one of the empty tables. "I picked up gifts for Olivia and Joseph, mostly."

"Uh, I caught sight of one of the books." The twitch in the corner of his mouth turned into a full-fledged grin as he set the cups on the table closest to the window. "I didn't know you were a romance reader."

"Inspirational romances are one of my few indulgences." She went to pull out her chair and suddenly he was there, holding it out for her. It was no easy task to hold her feelings still as he towered beside her, bringing with him the scent of winter snow and cozy pine. "It's an occupational hazard, I guess. And a family one. I grew up surrounded by books."

He waited while she settled into the chair and helped her to scoot it in. She was touched by the gesture. As if she didn't admire him enough. Jonah Fraser was a gentleman through and through.

"Ben said that your publishing company is one of the big ones. It's been in your family for generations."

"Yes. I don't work with books, though. I would probably be happier at my job if I did."

"Then what do you do exactly?" He moved away to take the chair on the far side of the table. "I know, you sit in a high corner office, taking meetings and delegating, don't you?"

"I'm more of a glorified bookkeeper."

"I don't believe that for one second."

"It's true. I spend my entire very long, sometimes twelve-hour workday with profit-and-loss statements, cost reports, production reports, projected earnings, monthly expenses, etcetera, etcetera. If they can make a spreadsheet on something, then it's on my desk."

"That doesn't sound like much fun."

"It isn't. Don't get me wrong. I am very thankful for my job and everything it allows me to afford for Mia." But there was the bookshop in the background, behind Jonah's shoulder, with the polished wood shelves and browsing customers and colorful book spines lined up carefully. There was that yearning again, at the bottom of her heart where she'd banished it. It wasn't the only yearning there. She did her best not to look directly at Jonah. It made that sweet and innocent longing she felt for him a little easier to ignore.

He studied her over the rim of his cup. "Tell me about your dreams, the ones you didn't follow."

She swirled her finger into the mountain of melting whipped cream. It was hardly a mannerly thing to do but she lifted a dollop of the sweet topping with her finger and licked it, the way she used to do when she was little. She'd spent too much time on lost dreams today and her spirit ached like a chipped tooth. "Dreams? I hardly remember them anymore."

"I know how that feels." He took a long sip and wiped the marshmallow mustache from his upper lip. "There's another thing we have in common."

Although he was smiling, it wasn't a real smile. He looked lost. It was the saddest look she'd ever seen on anyone. She remembered what he'd said about being a marine and serving the greater good. She wondered what had happened to bring him home and if it had something to do with his serious limp.

"What dreams have you lost?" she dared to ask.

He set his cup down on the table and stared into it. She could see the fall of his hair and the cowlick at the crown of his head. She didn't think he was going to answer her. Her heart skipped a beat. She was afraid he was going to get up and leave.

When he spoke, a dark emotion resonated in his baritone like a bell's final toll, an emotion that spoke of deep pain. "Remember when I said that life never turns out the way you expect?"

She nodded. She would never forget the day she'd first laid eyes on him. How the gray daylight had burnished him like a dream from her heart.

There she went, thinking of dreams again. Clearly, Jonah was not a dream meant for her as, she'd discovered, many dreams were not.

She cleared the disappointment from her throat. "Were you talking about being a soldier?"

Grief marked his handsome face. "I love my country. I'm proud to have served. It was what God called me to do."

And the leg injury? She clamped her lips together to hold the question in. She could feel the depth of his pain as if it were her own. She could read the shadows in his eyes and his strong heartfelt pain settled like a shroud over hers. He bowed his head and looked down at the whipped cream melting over the side of the cup.

What had happened to him? She wondered. She watched the news. She read newspapers. It was her job to keep up with current events and trends of books on the market. Her family's company had published several nonfiction accounts from soldiers' experiences in war.

She thought of all the tragedy Jonah could have seen with his own eyes. She thought of all the tragedy that could have happened around him in war. To him. And she remained silent, waiting. The last thing she wanted to do was to make him hurt more. She knew deep pain could be easier to manage if you kept a tight lid on it. It had to be dealt with one day, but now was clearly not the time. Nor, she suspected, was she the right one for him to tell.

So she waited, to allow him to wrestle the pain back down. She waited for him to say what he needed to say, if anything. Although he wasn't interested in her romantically and there were a dozen reasons why she shouldn't be interested in him, there *was* something there between them. Something she couldn't put her finger on. Some reason her heart kept feeling drawn inexorably by his.

He broke the silence with a bittersweet smile. "Here I've let the conversation take a turn for the worse. When I saw you, I came over because I had a few questions for you."

"For me?"

"Sure. I wanted to know how it's going with Ben."

Disappointment washed over her. As if she needed more proof he wasn't interested in her. Debra inwardly groaned. If there was something between them, then it was all on her side. Hadn't she been there before? It took all her strength to keep the memory of Mia's father at the back of her mind.

She cupped her hands around the cup of steaming hot chocolate for comfort. "Ben. That's a topic that's both complicated and as simple as can be."

"A paradox, huh? Explain, please."

Debra took one look at the compassion on Jonah's rugged face and gathered up a little more of her strength. "I came here only for Mia. The last few years have been difficult in our family with Mom's death and wrestling with that. She and I hadn't been on good terms for a long time. When Mia went off to school in Massachusetts in September, it divided us more than I imagined."

"You two seem close, despite that issue."

"Finding out about Ben has helped bring things back to the way they were between us. *Almost.*" Deb held back the more personal things Jonah probably didn't want to hear. About how the rift between her and Mia had begun to feel like the rift she'd had between her and her own mother through her teenaged years. Culminating in the painful, final rift that had changed their relationship forever.

She took a trembly breath. "Finding out about Ben was a shock. My mom was a very strict and devout Christian. We never knew this secret she was hiding. That she'd had a baby out of wedlock and had given him up for adoption. She was so proper, so unerring in her life as a wife and mother, that I simply can't imagine it, even now."

"It must be hard," he said quietly and with compassion. "You can't sit down and talk it out with her."

"Exactly. It's raised up more pain and old issues in a way that—" Hurt. She held back the word. She didn't want to be so honest with Jonah. Surely his interest in her answer concerned his friend and his boss, not her troubles. "Ben is wonderful. His wife and children are completely lovable. They already feel like family. I'm so glad Mia prodded me into visiting them."

"Caring about them is the simple part. I get that." Jonah took a long sip of chocolate and studied her with his wise, dark eyes. "What about the complicated part you mentioned? You've been through a hard time, I can see it."

His words knocked the breath out of her. Maybe this connection and what she felt between them was simply nothing more mysterious than the fact that they'd both been deeply hurt in different ways. Rain fell into everyone's life, as her mom used to say.

Maybe that was the reason she felt so drawn to Jonah and it was nothing more complicated than that. Relief breezed through her, making it easier to open up. After all, they were just two people sharing stories. That was all.

"Fine, but don't say I didn't warn you. It's complicated and personal."

"Hey, I'm a marine. I can handle anything."

She didn't doubt that. But how did she find the right words? "My brother and sister knew nothing about Ben. My mother never told us. There was not a hint. There was nothing to prepare us. Nothing to begin to make sense of her deception."

"She might not have known how to bring up something as painful as giving up a baby," Jonah suggested. "Wasn't she one of the people being blackmailed by Barnaby Harcourt?"

"Yes." She hurt for her mom.

"That had to have been terribly frightening for her—fearing the people she loved most might not understand." His compassion warmed his voice.

She was right about him. He had a big heart. A good heart. She admired him even more. "Those are exactly some of the things I wish I could talk to Mom about."

"There's no way to lay the past to rest between you. So it just keeps haunting you."

"Yes. Exactly." He understood. Debra blinked against the hot pressure pressing at her eyes. No one had seemed to understand. Not her sister, not her brothers and not even her father. She'd been alone with her feelings, struggling with them as they built and built. Until they began to harden like a husk inside her. She hadn't realized how much she'd craved a little understanding.

There was more of the story to tell. She studied the man before her, big and rugged-looking and as reliable as a wish. She knew he might understand.

She ran her finger over a pattern of the grain on the wooden table top. "Mom was a good wife and mother. When I was Mia's age, I wanted to grow up to be just like her. She seemed sure of every step she took. She didn't look right or left, she didn't wonder or worry. She took a stance, made a decision and that was it. Her faith was deep and unwavering. But one day everything changed between us."

"Tell me."

She couldn't look at him, trying to figure out the words to use. How did she explain how confused she felt? It left her torn up, the way she loved her mother dearly and at the same time, she was so angry for the lies. For the secrets. "I was her daughter. We were close. I told her all my secrets and sorrows. I don't understand why she didn't tell me hers when she had the chance. And believe me, when I was in college, she had the perfect chance to tell me."

She glanced between her lashes to peek at Jonah's response. To see if he caught on, or if she would have to talk about the time in her life that hurt all these years later.

"I can do the math." Jonah spoke carefully, his rugged baritone. "If Mia is thirteen, then you had to be fairly young when she was born."

"Yes. I—I wasn't married at the time." She focused on a knothole in the wood. It was easier to get the words out that way. "I was in college, in love and talking about marrying my first very serious boyfriend."

"So, you married him?"

Jonah's question surprised her like a slap to her face. Of course he would assume such a thing and that made it harder. Deep inside she could still feel the shattered illusions of the trusting, sheltered, naive college girl she'd been. A girl who saw only the good in the man she loved with all her soul.

She watched him through her lashes again so she could read his response and lowered her voice. "You're a minister's son. You might have a different opinion of me once I admit that, no, I didn't marry Jeff. I wasn't engaged. I was young and I went against the values I'd been raised with."

"Everyone makes mistakes."

"Even you?"

"Especially me."

She didn't believe it. He'd probably done nothing wrong in his life. He had a noble heart. "I let myself believe that being almost engaged wasn't much different than being married. We would get there eventually, right? But when I discovered I was going to have Mia, I learned there was a big difference."

"He didn't stand by you?"

"Stand by me? No." She had expected Jeff to reach out to her when, instead, he'd been horrified at the news. "He wasn't ready, that's what he said. He had his whole life ahead of him and he wasn't going to let me mess it up for him."

"That had to hurt you. I'm sorry you went through that."

She would always feel that wound in her heart. She would never forget the choice adjectives that Jeff had called her—*manipulative* had been the nicest of them. Words that had cut her down to the quick. She'd been so careful, yet it hadn't made a difference in the end. Too late, she realized the wisdom of the values she'd been raised with.

Jeff had simply rejected her and walked away, shattering more than her trust and her trusting heart. She'd never been in another romantic relationship. Until she'd met Jonah, she'd never wanted to even think about being in one.

Jonah broke the silence between them. "Do you think your mother should have told you her secret when you found yourself pregnant and alone, the way she had once been?"

"She was s-so harsh with me when I found out I was expecting Mia. She was so angry that I can still hear her yelling. *Angry* isn't the word. She was furious." Debra swallowed hard against the pain of the argument that had left her relationship with her mother in tatters for a decade. "After Jeff left me, I went straight to her. I needed my mom. I needed her. I thought she would stand by me."

"She didn't?"

Debra shook her head. "I knew she wouldn't approve of the poor judgment I'd shown, but I knew, deep down, she'd be there for me. When she wasn't, it felt like I'd lost the foundation of my world. Things were never the

same. Ever. I could never forgive her for for-
bidding me to take the easy way out and put
the baby up for adoption."

"Is that what you wanted?"

"I didn't know what I wanted right then. I just
needed to know that I wasn't alone. In the end,
for every day that passed after that moment, I
was. Mom wasn't there for me. Sure, she and
Dad didn't abandon me, but there was always
this wound between us. They kept me at a
distance. I did the same to them. I always felt
as if I had to make up for it but nothing could
make it right. No matter how hard I worked. No
matter how well I took care of Mia."

"Is that why you gave up those dreams you
wouldn't tell me about? Why you followed the
path your family wanted for you?"

"Yes. I'm fortunate to have the educational
opportunities I've had and I had a good job
waiting for me. It's given Mia the kind of life
I want for her. The kind of life I had growing
up. But I don't think I realized why I worked
so hard. Not until lately." At a loss, she shook
her head, held up her hands, torn apart by hurts
that could not be fixed.

She considered the man across the small
table from her. He looked deep in thought. He'd
been listening intently. But this isn't what he'd

been looking for when he'd bought her a cup of hot chocolate. "Sorry, that's been building up for a long time."

"Then I'm glad you told me." He smiled, showing his double dimples and his infinite kindness.

Her soul gave a little sigh.

He drained his hot chocolate and set the cup on the table. "That's quite a story you told me. You've been on your own ever since?"

"Raising Mia, yes. My family has been supportive over the years."

"You have done a fine job raising your daughter."

"I'm glad you think so." That little sigh turned into a bigger one. "You have to understand, this isn't about Ben. I know you care for him. He's your friend. He's been like a gift to my entire family. It's like getting a little bit of Mom back, in some way."

"I understand that." He gave the empty cup a push, as if to do something with his hands as he gave the matter some thought. "You want my take on things?"

"I have to admit I am wondering what you think of my long and very personal story."

He steepled his hands. "Have you ever considered that maybe your mom didn't mean to hurt you? In her own way, she was trying to protect you from what she went through in giving up a baby for adoption. That must be a kind of pain that never ends."

"But why the deception? She could have told me."

"Maybe it hurt too much. What kind of grief would that have been for her? To never hold that baby again. Never share the little moments of every day with him. Not watching over him while he grew up. She never knew what happened to him, if he was loved and safe or hurting and alone? She never knew what had become of him or even his name. And then the blackmailing on top of it? I can see how much your mom must have loved you, after losing her firstborn. What if she only meant to keep you from the same anguish? What if she feared losing you if she did tell you? I know you enough to see how she must have loved you."

Debra's eyes stung as she considered his words. Like a slap to the soul, she felt humbled before this great man, so full of compassion. He was right. From the moment the nurses had first placed Mia into her arms, a precious little bundle of sweetness swathed and blinking against the new sensation of light, an over-whelming wave of love had struck her like a tsunami, carrying her away with a devotion so powerful no other earthly force could be stronger.

What would it have felt like to have then given Mia away for adoption, thinking it would be best for her? Debra couldn't imagine it.

Worse, what would it be like if one day something tore her and Mia apart and they were never close again? Both would be like having her soul ripped out of her. Tears burned behind her eyes. Agony pounded through her. Agony her mother must have felt every day of her life.

"I just would have wanted her to love me enough to have been honest with me. It would have healed everything." She took a trembling breath, working at the knothole again. "Now it's too late."

"It's never too late. The power of prayer is an amazing thing."

"I keep hearing that." She couldn't help smiling at the irony. Maybe it *was* a sign from above. Maybe there was more to her being here in Chestnut Grove, the way Mia insisted there was. Deb was looking backward at her life and feeling the weight of that old sadness and something new. Something that felt suspiciously like hope.

She also noticed anew how truly handsome

Jonah was, dazzling inside and out. In the stillness and the sparkle of light from the Christmas window display, he looked as breathtaking as when she'd first set eyes on him. White twinkle lights graced him as if with a heavenly touch.

He pushed back his chair. "Well, I've got a book on hold to pay for. I'd best get going. I'm in the phonebook, if you feel the need to talk again. Good night, Debra."

Breathless, she could only watch as he quickly saluted her, turned and walked away. Being with him tonight was as if she'd spent her life in shadow and suddenly had stepped into the light.

Hours later, long after she was safely tucked away in her room at the bed-and-breakfast, the brightness in her heart remained and did not fade.

Chapter Seven

On Sunday morning, the Chestnut Grove Community Church looked picture perfect. Debra climbed out of her SUV, well bundled against the single-digit chill. Ice crunched beneath her boots as she closed the door. Her breath froze in the air, rising in puffs as she stepped up onto the sidewalk.

The scene was pretty enough for a Christmas card, Debra thought as she leaned her head back. The church's spire disappeared into the mist of snow. Peace filtered down with the sugary flakes and landed against her face.

The days were whizzing by; already it was Sunday. They had less than a week left here before heading home. That meant they only had six more days before Christmas. She was no longer in a hurry to leave this place, not that she wanted to think about the reason why. She was afraid that reason had everything to do with Jonah.

"Mom!" Mia bounced in place on the sidewalk, dressed in her Sunday best. "Hurry! I see Jonah."

Debra did her best not to scan the small knot of families disappearing inside the church. Talking to him the other night had made a difference. Peace seemed to cling to her as she spotted him in the crowd. She caught a glimpse of his navy blue jacket and the rugged cut of his profile before he disappeared inside the church.

"It's a sign, Mom."

Definitely a sign she should pay attention to, Debra mused as she caught Mia's hood and tugged it up over her head. "What's the sign this time?"

"I was just saying it to myself. I'm so happy, words are just bubbling out."

"So I see."

Mia swiped snow from her face. "Have you ever thought about getting married, Mom?"

Where was this coming from? "When would I find the time to get married? I have my hands full keeping up with my energetic and awesome daughter."

"Oh, Mom." Mia shook her head. "I'm praying for you. I think that's your only chance."

"I'm glad to know I'm such a hopeless case." Debra bit her bottom lip to hold back her amusement, but failed. Life was never dull around Mia.

"Do you think *they're* here yet? Olivia said she'd save a place for us. We've got to sit together."

"Oh, I know. Don't worry. There's their van, parked nice and close. They must have arrived earlier than we did."

Mia grabbed a hold of Debra's hand. "We've gotta invite them to all our regular stuff, now that we love them so much. When I talked to Uncle Brandon last night on the phone, he said we've *got* to invite the new branch of our family to all our stuff now."

"All our stuff?"

"You know. New Year's Day. How Granddad makes his super spicy turkey chili and we have snacks all day, you know, the junk food you won't let me have normally? And Aunt Lydia plays the piano and we all sing with her and the guys watch football? Don't you think Uncle Ben should come?"

The steps loomed up ahead and Debra found herself walking a little more slowly to savor this moment. It was as if the difficult events in her life had faded away and her relationship with Mia was back to the way it used to be. She felt as light as the snowflakes drifting from heaven.

The moment they stepped into the church, she found him. She wasn't trying to locate him in the crowd. She just looked toward the front of the church where a colorful stained-glass window filtered light over the beautifully aged wooden pews. Families and friends crowded together, chatting in the moments before the service started, and above all the voices she heard his cozy baritone.

He was standing near the front talking with a short, motherly-looking woman, who had red hair and freckles. Remembering Jonah's sister, Dinah, and how she'd looked very similarly, Debra supposed the woman was Jonah's mother. She looked like a cuddly, wonderful type of mom.

Across the crowded sanctuary the organ music began a sweet hymn and Jonah tensed, as if he were suddenly aware of her gaze. She jerked her eyes away and kept them solidly, on the wood floor at her feet, letting Mia guide the way to where Ben and his family were.

She didn't look up until she was safely seated in one of the pews beside Leah, and Jonah was no longer in her line of sight.

* * *

The service was over, but Jonah was full of as much turmoil as he'd been before worship started.

Frustrated, he swiped his hands over his face. Peace was a tough thing to find—and some days tougher than others. It looked like today might be one of those days. He'd gotten little sleep last night—again. His nightmares were a lot worse lately. And that wasn't all. Debra had been on his mind. The image of her, the closeness he'd felt to her and the personal pain she'd shared with him haunted him like his memories from his service in Iraq.

He had wounds from the past, as Debra did, but his were far different from hers and—worse—they were his own responsibility. He had no one to blame but himself. Grief hit him hard. He tugged at his collar, his tie suddenly too tight, and felt ashamed that he'd failed in a way that could never be made right.

He knew Debra was in the sanctuary, he'd spotted her earlier when she'd arrived with Mia. As much as he wanted to see her and find out if she was feeling better after their talk, he held back. His sister had asked him twice about Debra. She'd learned from Pamela, the bookstore owner, that he'd been seen with an attractive brunette there Friday night. His mother, bless her, had that hopeful sparkle in her eye, and if he walked over to talk to Debra, it would get the whole family talking.

He nodded to Zach Fletcher, the police detective on the Tiny Blessings case, his wife, Pilar, and their kids—Adrianna, Eduardo and the baby, Noah. Zach waved in acknowledgment and steered his happy family into the aisle toward the door. There was no mistaking the loving look shared between the man and his wife.

Glad for his friends, Jonah watched them go. Big mistake. Because it turned him in the direction where Ben was holding a bundled and sleeping Joseph and helping his wife into her wool coat. Sweet little Olivia was busily chatting a mile a minute with Debra, as if explaining some exciting thing, and Debra listened with total concentration.

His heart stalled in his chest. She had to be the loveliest woman he'd ever seen—inside and out. She amazed him, all that she'd accomplished and all that she'd faced. She'd built a secure life for her and her daughter. She wasn't just smart and classy and materially successful—she was successful where it mattered. He admired her one hundred percent.

"Jonah?" A cheerful voice came from behind

him. He spun around to see Debra's daughter. "I loved your dad's sermon. You are totally lucky to have a minister for a dad. You're totally cool!"

"Back at you, Miss Mia. I'm glad you liked the service." Cute kid. She'd obviously remembered his offer to meet his dad. "If it's all right with your mom, you can hang with me and I'll introduce you to my parents."

"Awesome!" Mia's eyes rounded. "I would love that. But first, I wanted to ask you for this huge favor."

"Name it, little lady."

"Uncle Ben said they can't go to brunch with us this morning cause they have to go to his brother's. Now, we were invited, but Mom said she didn't want to impose on all their family functions, which is like a major bummer. But we're still going to brunch at the Starlight Diner. Could you come join us there sometime this morning? I mean, it would really help my mom out."

"Now, do I look like I have a dunce cap on my head?" He gave her a wink so she knew that while he wasn't angry with her, he *was* onto her. "I can see what you're up to. You think I like your mom."

"You really should. She's nice, isn't she?" Mia focused her puppy-dog eyes on him.

He melted like an ice cube in Baghdad. "I'm refusing to answer that, because you're going to take anything I say the wrong way. You sent your mom to the bookstore when you knew I'd be there. Right?"

"Oooo-kay. That's true." Mia did look a little guilty but a little pleased, too. "But you helped my mom. She was so much happier when she came to pick me up that night. Plus, she's been humming ever since. *Humming.* She's been sad for a long time. Now she's not. Maybe you could talk to her some more. You know, 'cause it'll help her."

He knew when he was being snowed, but he didn't mind. He liked thinking he'd made a difference. Besides, he didn't have what it took to let Mia down. "I'll see you there, little lady."

"Oh, thank you! Thank you!" She whirled on her pretty boots, her tasteful dark blue dress swirling around her knees. She dashed down the aisle a few feet before she stopped, turned and giggled at herself. "How could I have forgotten? You were going to introduce me to your dad. Remember?"

Across the sanctuary, he caught sight of Debra watching him. Her hair was pulled back in a fancy braid and she looked like a perfect winter morning in a light gray dress that was both feminine and modest. She looked like everything good in the world, everything he was too afraid to wish for.

She gave a little finger wave and he could see that Mia had been telling the whole truth. Debra did look more radiant somehow, as if the shields that had been up when he'd first met her had dissolved, letting her inner beauty shine out more clearly.

He'd help her. That simple knowledge eased some of the turmoil inside him. A little peace shone into his troubled soul like a shaft of morning sun.

"Come meet my parents," he told her across the heads of the thinning congregation.

They met in the main aisle. The line of escaping worshippers was moving at a snail's pace toward the open front door. Jonah was vaguely aware that he knew most of the people around him, but the only face that mattered was Debra's. Her smile drew him forward.

"Mom!" Mia hurried up to her. "Look who I found."

"You just found him, did you? As if he were lost."

Mia groaned and took her mother by the hand. "Jonah said he'd introduce us to his dad, you know, the real cool minister? And he's gonna take Uncle's Ben's place."

"What exactly does that mean?"

"He's gonna come to brunch with us. Isn't that awesome?"

"Awesome." Debra blushed a little as she faced him, but she looked as if she were amused, too. "The real question is, Jonah, do you think joining us is awesome? I know how hard it can be to say no to Mia."

"I'm happy to do it. It isn't often I get the privilege of going to brunch with two such lovely ladies." It was easier to say that than the truth. Over her shoulder, he could see his mom finishing up a conversation with Douglas Matthews. She was on her way up the aisle. He figured he had a few minutes, tops, to prepare Debra for the oncoming onslaught. "There are some things you need to know before you meet my mom."

"She looks perfect." Debra brushed a few stray wisps of silky brown hair that had escaped from her braid from her eyes. "She looks like the kind of mom you could tell anything to and make a batch of cookies with after."

"That's my mom exactly, except she's not the best cook. Sometimes an even worse baker." Jonah steeled himself for the inquisition. "She's—"

Too. Late. He'd misjudged her approach and she caught hold of his elbow.

"Son, is this Ben's sister and her lovely daughter? I've heard so much about you, Debra and Mia. I can't tell you how happy I am that you came to our little church this morning."

And even happier, Jonah guessed, to find them with him. "Debra, Mia, I'd like you to meet my mom, Naomi."

"Lovely to meet you, Mrs. Fraser." Debra accepted Naomi's hand.

Jonah's mother, being her typical loving self, wasn't happy with a handshake, so she wrapped Debra in a hug. Already she was smiling ear to ear. Apparently Debra met with her approval. "Goodness, you can't know how we've looked forward to meeting you, Debra. You, too, Mia, dear. Oh, aren't you adorable? Why, we've all known Ben since he was a little guy. The Cavanaughs are some of our dearest friends."

"Ben and his family certainly speak well of you and your husband. Mia has been dying to come to one of your husband's services, right, sweet pea?"

"Yep. It was so totally awesome. Mrs. Fraser, it's lovely to meet you." Mia was obviously trying hard to hold back her enthusiasm. "I love your church. It's awesome. It's really old, right?"

Jonah watched his mom "ahh" in adoration. She was clearly completely charmed by Mia and he knew exactly what his mother was thinking. He hadn't been a member of the Fraser family all his life without picking up a thing or two.

As his mom answered Mia's question about the church, talking about the eighteenth-century construction and the original wood-work and the historic cemetery out back, Jonah touched Debra's elbow to get her attention. The fine wool of her coat felt like velvet against his rough fingertips.

"Mom has her sights on you, so watch out." Jonah kept his voice low, leaning close so only Debra could hear. "My mother is fully cogni-zant of our last two rendezvous."

"Is that military vernacular for the tree-lighting ceremony and our bookstore meeting?"

"Exactly. Hey, I see that. You're trying not to laugh."

"Who's laughing?" Debra did her best to hold down her mirth, but the truth was, she felt so light. Weightless. As if the burdens weighing her down for the last thirteen years were starting to lift. She'd actually enjoyed the service and the only way to explain that was she'd misplaced her cynicism. Not that she expected it to last, but she was enjoying the moment. "I didn't know that my having two cups of hot chocolate with you qualifies as a big deal."

"Trust me. Big deal." Jonah ambled slowly at her side. His limp looked a little worse today. "When I was in Force Recon, I couldn't begin to top her ability to gather covert information. My mom could outdo the CIA and military intelligence combined."

"I'll be on my best behavior. I promise." She lay her hand on his, it felt like a natural thing to do. "We don't want your family to get the wrong idea."

"Exactly. Not that it will stop them, but I thought it was only fair to warn you."

"So, you are one of the good guys."

He winced and withdrew from her touch. "Sorry, far from good. I'm too flawed for that."

She wasn't able to argue for the line at the door had moved forward again and there was Reverend Fraser, taking her hand in a warm greeting.

"Debra Watson. No introduction is necessary." The warm, fatherly minister had a smile and a manner to match. "I've heard so much about you. Welcome. I hope you enjoyed this morning's service."

"I did. It has been a long time since a service has touched me so much." It was the truth, she realized with a startle. Maybe it was the historical, breathtaking structure and simple design of the church, but she felt authentic and peaceful here. "Our home church in Baltimore is a little more ornate, but I think this feels a little closer to heaven."

"I like to think so, too." Reverend Fraser had a hint of Jonah's smile and the same straight, unerring nobility of spirit.

Must be a family trait, and, she supposed, one that was rock-solid. Good to know, not that anything could come of her wishing, but a girl never knew what was around the bend. Today she felt so light, anything could happen. "Jonah has been kind enough to befriend us."

Mia piped in. "Yeah, Jonah is totally cool, and he's going to brunch with me and my mom."

"Well, isn't that just fine?" Naomi's pleasantly round face pinkened with pleasure. "Don't let us keep you, then. Debra, you must come to dinner with us before you leave. I'm looking forward to getting to know you and your beautiful daughter better."

Mia, unable to contain her excitement, spoke

first. "We'd love that, Mrs. Fraser. We really, really, *really* would."

Debra internally groaned. Mia was simply being Mia—she loved everyone and this was the minister and his family and faith was very important to her. But what about Jonah? She could plainly read on Naomi's face the hopes for her son. Didn't every loving mother want her grown child to be married and happily settled?

Before she could think of something to gently point out the truth to Naomi—that Jonah was certainly and most definitely not romantically interested in a mother with a teenaged girl, Jonah broke in.

"We'd best get to the diner. Mom, I'll talk to you when I get home." He shot his mother a meaningfully glance.

Naomi, such a dear, gave a "tsk" and waved her son on his way. "Go, then. Have a lovely time with Debra. It was so very *wonderful* to meet both of you."

After saying goodbye, Debra let Jonah lead her through the high doorway and into the frosty winter day. Snow fell like blessings, so sweet and plentiful, mantling the world.

For the first time in a long while, Debra felt renewed. Centered. At peace. She followed

Mia down the steps toward the street crowded with departing cars. She was able to let her troubles go and enjoy the crisp, clean day, the beauty of the snowfall and the friendly company of the man at her side.

Across town, Lynda Matthews unclasped the diamond-studded wristwatch her husband had given her as a showy gift. Her hand was unsteady and her fingers fumbled with the clasp. She was afraid. She set it on the kitchen counter and sighed. There, that was the last thing. She wanted to take nothing of Douglas's—or anything that he had given her—with her to remind her of the lie she'd been living. Or of the pretense he played like the actor and liar he was and the shambles he'd made of their marriage.

Now that she'd carefully weighed everything and made her decision there was nothing to do but to leave. It hadn't been an easy decision, but Douglas had helped her make it. She hadn't truly believed he would go too far. She should have stuck with her safety plan. She should have left before he'd hurt her so badly and in front of her son.

"Come along, Logan." She held out her hand. "Don't forget your fuzzy bear."

"Yes, Mommy." Her sweet little boy plodded

along the kitchen cabinets, head down, his black hair falling to hide his eyes. He needed a haircut, but that would be taken care of in Richmond. He halted in front of her, looking up at her with his serious blue eyes. "Where's D-Daddy?"

"He's busy this morning. Don't you worry. It'll be just you and me going for a ride today. We can get a drive-through cheeseburger meal, the way you like." She took his little hand in hers.

"Okay." His little shoulders slumped. Not even the prospect of his favorite fast food would cheer him up.

No child should wear sadness like a shirt. That's how she knew she was doing the right thing. She still had a lot of worries. But it was the pastor's words she remembered now. He'd told her that abuse is a sin.

She grabbed her purse. She'd already slipped two small suitcases into the back of the minivan. They were ready, leaving with only a few clothes and Logan's most beloved toys. She plucked her keys from the counter and caught a reflection of her face in the mirror on the wall. Fresh bruises stained her jaw and cheekbone, the reason why she'd not attended church this morning.

Douglas had handed her this blessing in

disguise, in a way. He watched her so closely, but with the importance of his upcoming Christmas show on the local network he felt he could not miss Sunday service. She slid the van key from the key ring and left the other keys next to the diamond watch.

She was done with Douglas Matthews.

Noting the time, she realized church was just getting out. Douglas would be heading to another one of his all-important meetings with that agent of his, pretending to be the good man he was not. He'd probably be calling in to check on her in a while. Best to leave now.

As she let the door click shut behind her and buckled Logan into his car seat, she wondered how long it would take him to realize she was gone, truly gone, for good.

Please, Lord, she prayed. *Please understand and forgive me. I just want to be safe. I want my son to be safe.*

She didn't know if God heard her. With trembling fingers, she eased her sore body into the driver's seat and turned the ignition key. The van's gas tank was full, there were snacks and sandwiches in a little insulated carrier on the floor to see them to Richmond where her family would take her in.

She felt like a scared rabbit fleeing like this,

but the weight of her deep unhappiness lifted as she drove down the driveway. She did not look into her rearview mirror once. Ahead, that's where she kept her eyes and her thoughts.

She never wanted to think of Douglas Matthews again.

Chapter Eight

Starlight Diner was packed. Jonah knew nearly every person in there, including Douglas Matthews who was standing in the entryway, unaware he was blocking the entrance, furiously dialing his cell phone. He was an odd one, although Jonah couldn't say exactly why. He shielded Debra and Mia from him and the jostling crowd.

"Looks like we'll be lucky to get a table," he told her. Maybe that was for the best, considering this probably wasn't the kind of place Debra and Mia were used to.

"This is so cool!" Mia hopped in place as she glanced around at the '50s-style decor. "It's like retro."

"How fun." Debra sounded as if she meant it. "And the food smells wonderful."

"It's one of the best places for brunch in town." He noticed a few friendly faces—his buddies, mostly—watching him with shock. Considering he hadn't dated at all since he'd been honorably discharged, he'd figured being seen with a woman like this was bound to get folks talking.

Luckily there was a booth near the back against the long bank of windows. Jonah felt a little better with his back to the wall and out of the line of sight of all those friends of his who were bound to be asking questions later.

"Hi, hon." Sandra Lange whipped out her order pad, her green eyes traveling from him to the lovely woman and her daughter across the Formica tabletop. "I heard from Ross you had yourself a new girlfriend."

Jonah watched Debra flush to a rosy red. Debra was cute. Real cute.

She fumbled with the laminated menu on the table in front of her. "Oh, no. I'm Ben Cavanaugh's sister and this is my daughter—"

"I know who you are." Sandra winked and poised her pen on the pad. "My girl, Kelly, is married to one of Jonah and Ben's good friends. You have to know we've all been rooting for him to find happiness. You plannin' on staying in town long?"

Jonah didn't want Debra to feel any more on the spot than she already was, so he cut in. "Debra, Mia, this is Sandra, the owner of this fine dining establishment. She makes the best eggs Benedict in the state."

Debra elegantly folded a wisp of hair behind her ear, her gaze meeting his. Her cheeks were still pink with color, but her blush was beginning to fade. "Then eggs Benedict it is and a cup of tea. If I have this straight, then the crib Jonah was making for Ross and Kelly's baby would also be for your grandbaby."

"Oh, it surely is. You want to see a picture?" Beaming, the proud grandmother pulled a plastic packet of photos from one of her many apron pockets. A solitaire diamond winked on her left ring finger. "Cameron came a little early, three whole weeks, but he and his mama are doin' great now. You may not have heard all the goings-on. I'll let Jonah fill you in. Isn't he a sweetheart?"

"A complete sweetheart." Debra leaned in to study the snapshots. "He looks so tiny."

"He's already grown a bunch. He's thriving." Sandra glanced at the pictures before she lovingly tucked them away. "I see you noticing my new ring."

"Is it new?" Debra asked. "It's a lovely

princess cut. That's a very fine quality diamond. Congratulations. Who's the lucky man?"

"I would be the lucky one, seeing as my husband-to-be is over there. I've never been happier." She nodded toward a familiar man a few tables away. Debra recognized him as the man who played Santa at the tree lighting at the Mayor's mansion. "Now, what'll you have, darlin'?"

Mia was biting her lip, uncharacteristically quiet. She'd been studying the baby pictures over her mom's shoulder. Now she slid back into the seat. "Can I please have a glass of orange juice and what Santa Claus over there is having?"

Two booths over, Tony Conlon was sipping a cup of tea. He had a big stack of blueberry pancakes and sausages on the table in front of him. The man really did look like Santa Claus, even without the red suit. Maybe it was the white beard and his merry look.

"Pancakes it is, darlin'. I'll be right back with your drinks. You let me know if you need anything, you hear?" Sandra sauntered off, pausing at Tony's table to check on him. The look the two shared was pure love.

How wonderful to see that love could come

into a person's life even later in the game, Debra thought. Then she noticed the man at the booth on the other side of Tony. The black-haired, perfectly coiffed man looked familiar to her and he was rudely signaling for the waitress.

Jonah must have noticed where she was looking. "That's our local celebrity. Douglas Matthews. Do you know him?"

"I know of him." She'd never met him, but she didn't think she wanted to meet him now. Douglas Matthews looked agitated as he exchanged words with Sandra. She knew her publishing company had considered a six-figure book deal with the talk-show host, but her brother Brandon, the president of the company, had decided to pass after a few questionable pictures had made their way into the paper. "It doesn't look as if he's having a good day."

"No, it doesn't." Jonah nodded at another table at the other side of the diner. One of his friends, probably. "That's Ross and Kelly Van Zandt. Sandra's daughter. Kelly was in a car accident not too long ago when she was pregnant with Cameron. That's why he was a little early."

"How scary. Sandra mentioned both mom and baby are okay."

"Kelly broke her wrist and went into early

labor, but everything's fine now." Jonah took a sip of water. "Someone tampered with her car. Her brakes gave out."

"Tampered with? Intentionally?" Debra glanced over her shoulder to the happy little family on the far side of the restaurant. They were hard to see, but there was no mistaking the husband's dark handsome look and Kelly's golden sweetness.

Shock filtered through her. "Kelly's the one who runs the adoption agency," Debra remembered. "What kind of man would tamper with a pregnant woman's car? Knowingly cause an accident? I can't imagine such a thing. Someone like that, well, I suppose he'd do anything. He must not have a conscience. Is she still in danger?"

"We don't know the answer. It could have been more serious. They were lucky."

"They have a baby, too," Mia broke in, biting her bottom lip, her forehead furrowed with thought.

Uh-oh, Debra mused. *I know that look.* She had no idea what the girl was thinking now. "I'm glad mom and baby are fine. It seems like a lot of your friends are starting families. Ben and Leah have little Joseph. Everywhere we turn, it seems there's another one."

"It's nice to see my friends happy." Jonah fidgeted a little.

"I'm sorry. I should have known. Talking about babies makes all bachelors uncomfortable. I think it's some kind of a rule."

"Maybe." Jonah chuckled. "I'm getting used to it. Did you notice how my mother jumped to conclusions when she met you?"

"I saw. She was wonderful. I have one question about her."

"You want to know how a big rough guy like me ended up with such a sweet little mom, right?"

"Those weren't the words I would use, but, yes, something like that. She looks like a soft touch."

"I told you. Mom should have been CIA. She's a softy, but she's stalwart. I'm blessed to have the parents I do."

"I was thinking the same thing—"

"Jonah." Mia leaned her elbows on the edge of the table, although she had better manners than that. Just as she knew better than to interrupt, but she did it anyway. "Do you like kids?"

"What do you think?" He shot a glance at Debra, the molten-gold strands in his dark eyes shimmering with mirth.

"I think you like 'em." Mia decided with definite certainty. "Where do you live?"

"I've got an apartment not too far from here. Is that okay with you, Miss CNN?" Jonah paused as Sandra approached and set down the juice and two cups of steaming tea. She promised the food would be right out before she hurried away.

Mia didn't miss a beat. "How come you don't have a house?"

"Because it's just me. A house is a lot of space for one guy."

"Then you like houses."

"Sure. Who doesn't like houses?" Jonah pushed the tray of condiments in Debra's direction so she could use the honey first.

She couldn't say why it was the little gestures that touched her so deeply. Maybe because it was something her father would have done for her mother; something Mia's father had never done for her, even before their breakup.

Mia didn't blink as she kept asking questions. "How come you're not married?"

"No one's said yes."

"Do you have a Christmas tree yet?"

All right, that was enough. Jonah looked amused, but Debra decided to rescue him anyway. "Mia, I'm sure Jonah doesn't want to be under fire. It's Sunday. We're supposed to be taking it easy, according to the Bible. It's a day of rest, right?"

"So close, but so far away," Mia sighed with a hint of drama, as if her burden were truly great. "I finally get you to mention the Bible, but you just don't get it, Mom. I try and I try."

"You ham." Debra wrapped her arm around her daughter and drew her close into a hug. She gave her a kiss on the forehead. She dearly loved her little girl. "I miss you when you're away at school."

"Does this mean I don't have to go back?"

"You know the answer to that." She held onto her girl for a few moments longer. "Why don't you give the question-and-answer session a rest? On the news shows they at least take a commercial break. Don't you think Jonah deserves the same?"

"Ah, but, Mom, I've got so many question I can't hold them all in."

Debra had to admit she had a lot of questions, too. She spied Sandra coming with their loaded plates. Ah, a negotiating point. "If Jonah doesn't mind, why don't you say the blessing?"

"Okay, but I've still got questions."

To his credit, Jonah looked not only amused, but caring. "Don't worry about it, little lady." He tugged at his tie to loosen it a notch. "If we're all going to be friends, we might as well really get to know each other."

"Exactly!" Mia clasped her hands together. "I especially want you and my mom to be friends. She's such a hopeless case."

Debra couldn't help laughing, lighthearted, as Sandra set the delicious-looking meal in front of her.

The snowfall had begun to taper off while they were enjoying brunch. So by the time they walked out the door Jonah held open for them and onto the sidewalk, it was like being greeted by a picture from a child's Christmas storybook.

Beauty was everywhere. Light, spun-sugar flakes sifted lazily from a white-gray sky. The fresh sheet of snow seemed to ice over the world's imperfections, turning telephone wires and bare tree branches and even the soiled dredges of snow at the sides of the street a perfect wonderful white.

"You sighed," Jonah pointed out as he joined her on the sidewalk.

"Did I?" Debra felt as if she hardly knew herself any longer. This trip was changing her. Discovering the truth was changing her. "This is a lovely town. It must be sweet to live here. No hustle and bustle, no horrible commuter traffic. There's something in the air. Everything holds such promise."

"It is a great place to live, but then again, I'm biased." Jonah stuffed his hands in his coat pockets. "Chestnut Grove has its troubles like anyplace. Some crime. Desperate people. People who make bad choices. We're lucky we have much smaller problems as a community, over all, than other cities."

"I suppose I'm just being nostalgic for some kind of ideal life that no one has." Debra didn't know how to describe the tangle of want and longing in her heart. "I guess sometimes I wish I'd followed a different path. I see Mia—"

Where had Mia gone? Debra paused to check over her shoulder, but she shouldn't have been surprised to see her little girl with her face tilted up to the heavens, letting the snow land on her face.

Debra cleared her throat. "Mia's starting to wear me down. I used to be a lot like her at that age. Lately I've been wondering where that Debra went."

"I can see her."

His words cut deep, jarring her all the way to the bottom of her soul. It took all her effort to keep walking casually. This didn't feel casual. That tiny light of affection for him within her brightened a notch, so sweet and adoring she knew it had to show.

Thank the heavens for the snow that was a veil between them. Maybe he wouldn't notice.

Jonah held out his hand, palm up. "Your keys?"

Without thinking, she handed them over. Snowflakes tinkled and tapped as Jonah crunched to her SUV, unlocked the door with the remote, started the engine and checked under the driver's seat. He pulled out the long ice scraper. He flashed her a grin. "I knew it would be there. You're an organized woman."

She shouldn't be surprised that he was clearing her windows and scraping at the sheen of ice that had melted onto the glass. "Your limp is worse when the weather is colder and damper."

He kept his back turned, reaching to clean off the middle of the windshield. "I don't let it bother me. I got lucky, considering."

Voices broke in, cutting off her next question. A family tumbled out of the diner's door, their conversations light and happy. Debra bit her bottom lip, holding back the question, but the words bubbled inside her. He'd been a marine. She'd been wondering if he'd been injured on active duty. Now she knew, without words, that he had.

She'd read enough and watched news enough

to understand what that meant. He'd been hurt over there, and, in reconsideration of his comment, she understood that he meant others hadn't been so lucky. He'd seen others die.

Poor Jonah. All her own worries faded, except for one—her all-out concern for this good man.

Jonah didn't look up as he swept the dregs of snow and ice from the windshield. "You two lovely ladies go on, get in where it's warm."

"It doesn't feel right to leave you out here in the cold."

"I don't mind." The flecks in his eyes warmed like liquid gold and he stopped what he was doing to hold the door open for her.

Debra felt cozy from his thoughtfulness, then the diner's front door smacked open, startling her. For a moment, she almost forget they weren't alone. There was that Matthews fellow again. He didn't look too happy as he checked the screen on his cell phone and dialed furiously. What troubled Debra more was that her daughter was noticing the enraged looking man. His obscene curse echoed in the parking lot.

Shocked by the celebrity's behavior, Debra held out her hand to Mia's shoulder. "Hurry up. In the car, kid."

"What's wrong with him, Mom?"

"I don't know, but there's no excuse for that."
Debra steered her daughter to the safety of the
SUV, keeping an eye on Douglas Matthews.

He appeared very agitated and his perfectly
polished appearance had started to frazzle. His
dark hair was mussed and his face twisted in
anger as he snapped off his phone and stared
at it. She got Mia's door closed just in time.
Another curse echoed across the parking lot.

Jonah had straightened. "Matthews. This is
a family establishment."

The man answered with an even worse curse,
yanked open the door to his luxury vehicle and
threw the phone in a temper into the passenger
compartment. Debra saw the fury on Jonah's
face—he was being protective of her and Mia.
But Douglas dove into his car in a hurry, shut
the door and started the engine with a loud roar
before Jonah could do anything.

"I'm sorry you had to hear that." A muscle
tensed in his jaw. Next to a man like Douglas
Matthews, Jonah Fraser looked like a dream.
He opened her door for her. "Thanks for letting
me tag along. I had a good time."

"I did, too. We enjoyed your company. We
should do it again. Ah, you should come
tomorrow night. To dinner at Ben's. I'm
cooking for everyone." The impulsive words

tumbled out before she could stop them. Impulse was not usually her style. When Jonah grinned, she knew she'd done the right thing.

He shook the wetness off the scraper and deposited it neatly on the back floor mat. "I'll think about it."

Mia twisted against her seat belt to chime in, "Dinner's at seven. I'm going to help with the cooking, so you gotta come. Promise?"

"I can't say no to you, Miss Mia."

"Yeah, I know. Why do you think I asked?"

"I'll bring a pie." He shut the back door with a click. "Do you two have any suggestions? Chocolate? Banana?"

"My mom's favorite is lemon meringue."

What were the chances? His, too. "Lemon it is. I'll see you tomorrow for dinner."

"Awesome." Mia made a punch in the air and dropped back into her seat.

Debra's window whizzed down, revealing her flushed face, sparkling eyes and dazzling smile. "Now the pressure's on. I'll try not to burn anything."

"If you do, I won't notice. Deal?"

"Deal." She put the SUV in gear. "Thanks, Jonah. I'm looking forward to it."

He waited while the SUV eased out of its spot, remembering what Mia had said earlier.

You helped my mom. She was so much happier when she came to pick me up. Maybe you could talk to her some more. Debra did look better, lighter somehow, as if she'd laid some of the pain of the past to rest.

I wish I could, Jonah thought longingly as he spotted Mia waving at him enthusiastically through the window. Mia was special. Too bad he liked her mother so much. Debra was… perfect. Exactly the kind of woman he'd always used to pray he would find.

But that was before Iraq. Reality hit him low and hard like a snowplow. Jonah hung his head, overwhelmed by shame. Like the frigid winter wind, guilt froze him to the marrow.

When he looked up, the taillights of Debra's SUV were small points of red on Main Street and then gone. He stared into the pure falling snow and felt ashamed. There were things he'd done, things he was responsible for, that he could never forget or make up for.

He wished he could. He wished forgiveness were possible. Thinking of those he'd failed, he didn't know how God could ever forgive him. One thing was sure, he could not forgive himself. He didn't deserve to love a wonderful woman like Debra or to be responsible for anyone again.

Weighed down by a ton of regret, Jonah dug his keys from his pocket and unlocked his truck. Sunday may be a day of rest, but he couldn't stand all this thinking and feeling. He had the foot and sideboards of Mia's bed to finish. Yes, that's what he'd do. He'd work the afternoon and evening through to keep his hands and mind busy. Work always helped to keep the memories at bay.

Douglas Matthews drove through the expensive development at the edge of town, his heartbeat racing and his anger rising. He couldn't reach her. Again. Lynda better have a good excuse for not answering the phone. She was supposed to spend her time seeing to his needs and keeping things running smoothly so he could put every ounce of his energy and talent into furthering his career. Why couldn't she see that? Because of her, he'd been too upset for his meeting. She was the reason his agent hadn't shown.

He'd had to sit in that tacky diner alone. At least he had the chance to see Ross Van Zandt in action. Acting like the good Christian family man, when the truth was he'd made a threat he couldn't keep.

That shabby P.I. couldn't find his way out of a cardboard box and he certainly wasn't good enough to outsmart Douglas Matthews. Ross Van Zandt had no evidence—and never would. Douglas would make certain of that. He'd sent one message—and it seemed to have worked. Ross had made threats—but it was hot air. Douglas had no problem sending another message, if that became necessary.

Smugly satisfied, he slowed down to take the turn into his driveway, bringing his property into sight. A fresh layer of snow glazed the lawns and along the impressive roofline of his house, so it was hard to tell at first what was missing.

The minivan.

A terrible foreboding turned cold in his gut. What was going on? Douglas stopped the car and launched out of the seat. It was no illusion. He stared in disbelief at the empty space where Lynda's minivan was supposed to be. Where had she gone? She was supposed to be home putting herself together. She had a lot to make up for lately. She was always setting off his temper.

Now this. What was he going to have to do to make her understand?

His cell phone went off. He slammed the garage door and dug the phone out of his pocket. It had to be Lynda. Horrible fury momentarily blinded him as he hit the answer button. Whatever she was out doing, he was going to make sure she learned her lesson. She just didn't learn. "Lynda?"

"No, Doug." It was Rob, his agent. "I'm returning all five of your voice messages."

Rob sounded a little too superior. Douglas gnashed his teeth but got his temper under control. There was a lot at stake. "You stood me up at the diner. I was… concerned."

Furious. Insulted. Ready to go shopping for a better agent. A top agent. One who had enough guts to close the network deal.

Rob cleared his throat. "The weather held me up, but after your last few messages, I'm concerned about you. You need to behave more professionally, Douglas. This is the reason we're having trouble taking you national."

That was rich. Red flashed before his eyes. "The reason I'm not hosting my own national show right now is because you're not aggressive enough."

"I'm not the one who was caught womanizing—"

"I told you that was nothing!"

"The threats you've made to my secretary."

"She wouldn't put my calls through!"

"The messages you've left today could be

taken as threatening. If I didn't know you better, Douglas, I would have to advise you to find other representation."

The red staining his vision turned crimson. Rage vibrated through him like a taut bow. "It's not my fault. I'm under a lot of stress. If you could get this deal closed, I would be better."

"Let's take it a day at a time. I'll call you in a few days. And, Douglas, maybe you ought to talk to someone. Like your pastor."

Before Douglas could set him straight, the connection went dead. Who did this joker think he was dealing with? He was Douglas Matthews. And where was Lynda? This was her fault. She had best get back soon, or—

He'd yanked open the front door and his hard, uneven breathing echoed in the silent house. His footsteps echoed long and deep, bouncing off the cathedral ceilings and imported marble. He noted the housework hadn't been done. The kitchen dishes were still in the sink.

Then he spotted the jewelry on the counter— her everyday jewelry. The diamond studded watch he insisted she wear was tossed on the counter next to her wedding ring.

Her wedding ring.

He didn't need to tear through the house to

figure out she'd left him. She'd probably packed a few things—things he'd bought her and the boy—and left him. She'd taken their son.

What was this going to do to his image? A curse tore from his throat. Blind with rage, he grabbed the first thing he came to—the stool at the breakfast bar—and threw it as hard as he could. It crashed through the window with a satisfying smash.

In the cozy warmth of their adjoining rooms, Mia knelt beside her bed, her hands clasped as she said her bedtime prayers while Debra waited in the doorway, leaning against it, struck by how thankful she was for her daughter. They'd been apart since September because of school, except for a few weekends and holidays at home, and that time was lost. Debra suddenly felt it sorely. Mia was changing, growing up a little more day by day, and so fast.

As she knelt, fervently praying, she looked a little taller, her face a little leaner and more mature. Mia whispered, "Amen," and hopped into bed.

Holding back her feelings, Debra stepped into the room. "You were praying pretty earnestly."

"That's how you're supposed to pray, Mom."

"I know." Knowing where this was about to lead, Debra slid onto the edge of the mattress and tucked the covers beneath Mia's chin. She might not feel as cynical about faith right now, but that didn't mean she felt ready to discuss it. "You want to do some more of our Christmas shopping tomorrow?"

"We'd better. Can we park downtown and wander through all the shops? I've been dying to do that." Mia propped herself up on one elbow to plump her pillow right before collapsing back onto it. Dark circles had worked their way beneath her eyes and her lids were drooping, but she was still buzzing with excitement from the evening. "Didn't we have the best day?"

"The best. Because I got to spend it with you." Debra brushed the hair out of Mia's face. "You were right. It's good thing that we came here to get to know our new family."

"*What?* I can't believe you said that."

"I'm cautious when it comes to making changes—"

"I'll saaaay." Mia stifled a yawn. "So, does that mean we can stay for Christmas?"

"Your grandfather is expecting us for Christmas dinner."

"Yeah, but that's at dinnertime on Christmas

Day. We could have Christmas morning here and then drive back home and still be there in time. Please?"

"We'll see about staying until Christmas Eve, at least." Debra loved seeing her child so happy.

"Good, because there's so much I have to do. I want to see the Christmas Eve services at the church. Jonah's father is the minister, you know, so we can go with Jonah, too."

"You're just full of plans, aren't you, sweetheart?"

"Yep. I'm praying hard so they'll come true. I just want a real family, Mom."

"I know you do." How could she fault her daughter for that? It *was* like a blessing to have this gift of Ben and his family to add to the Watson clan. She could no longer argue that truth.

Mia struggled against an even bigger yawn. "Olivia's lucky. It would be great to have a dad and a little brother. No, I'd want a sister. A little sister who's just like me."

"Which would make her perfect." Debra didn't know what else to say. That's all she had wanted, too, but it had never happened for her—love, marriage, the whole family thing. This wasn't the way she'd imagined her life to be long ago.

She wished she could see such a happy and lovely future as easily as Mia could. There was so much she wanted for her daughter. So much her own heart ached for. Sweet love for her daughter left her weak, as always, but strengthened her, too.

Debra smoothed away the wrinkles that had settled into Mia's forehead. "Sleep well, sweet pea. You have another big day tomorrow."

She kissed Mia's cheek and stood to turn off the bedside lamp. Darkness fell like a hush in the cozy room. The slab of light falling through the doorway to the adjoining room guided her as she made her way. By the time she closed the door, Mia was already fast asleep.

Her own room was cozy, lit by matching lamps flanking the bed on small antique tables and another by the overstuffed chair in the corner. As she went in search of the book she was reading, she straightened up the room as she went. Her thoughts kept going over the day. At church. At the diner. Talking with Jonah in the snowy parking lot. Thoughts of him brought peace to her spirit.

She was looking forward to spending more time with him tomorrow. It had been a long time since she'd felt this happy. She kicked off her shoes, curled up in the chair, opened her book and let the promise of happily-ever-after carry her away.

Chapter Nine

Ross opened the door of Pamela Lansbury's Christian bookstore. The shop was busy with Christmas shoppers. Both cashiers were working away at a long line of customers with gifts to purchase. Not a good sign. He hoped Pamela had time to talk with him now. He'd been so energized by Naomi Fraser's e-mail that he'd come straight here. Maybe he should have called.

"Ross." Pamela found him, waltzing into sight with an armful of devotionals she must have been shelving. "How lovely to see you. Tell me, how is your son getting along?"

"He's perfect." Ross remembered how terrified he'd been and filled with protective rage when he'd first seen his son in the neonatal unit at the children's hospital. "Can I speak with you alone?"

She looked a little surprised and glanced at the front. "I suppose the girls can handle things just fine for a few moments."

"It won't take long. I need your help."

"Is this about the Tiny Blessings investigation?" Pamela led the way to the back door marked Employees Only. "I saw your statement on the news a while back. You need to capture that man, Ross, whoever he is, before he hurts someone else."

"I will." He would not fail. As soon as the door closed, he patted the folded pages in his coat pocket. "I was wondering if you remember a young woman who worked for you once a long time ago. Her name was Wendy Kates."

"Oh, that dear girl." Pamela face fell. She looked deeply sad. "Wendy was the sweetest thing. It was terrible what happened to her, dying in childbirth."

Ross realized that Pamela didn't know the full truth about Wendy's death—or, murder, as he suspected. It was difficult keeping his emotions under wrap. "How well did you know her?"

"As well as anyone could, I guess. She just showed up one day, a little black and blue. She said her father had thrown her out of the house and she was obviously pregnant. I took her in, my heart broke for her. I don't think she had a friend in the world, so I let her stay in the little apartment above my garage."

Ross wasn't surprised to learn that Wendy had been battered. It was a pattern with some men, a terrible pattern of violence and brutality. "Surely Wendy confided in you. Do you know who the father of her baby was?"

"She only called him Douggie. I don't know if it was a first name or a last name or just a pet name she had for him. I felt so sorry for her, all alone like that."

"Are you sure she didn't know anyone else in town?"

"I don't think she knew many people in town. I kept trying to encourage her to go to church with my husband and me, but she resisted. She was afraid of being judged, I think. At least that poor baby was adopted by a nice family." The intercom in the overhead speaker came on, paging her. She sighed. "I'm sorry. I have to get back on the floor. Did you need anything else?"

"You've been a great help, Pamela." Ross followed her through the door. "I'd appreciate it if you don't mention this to anyone. Not even your husband. Can I have your word?"

"Of course. This is exciting to be a part of

your investigation. If I think of anything else, I'll call you." Pamela led the way into the hustle-bustle of the shop. "Good luck, Ross. I hope you get him."

"I will." Ross felt certain of it now. Douggie. Another piece of the puzzle. It fit very nicely with the initials he'd found—L.M. Several prominent families in town had last names that started with the letter *M*. Matthews was on that list of names.

Douglas Matthews. The Matthews were a prominent family. Douglas had always been and still was the town's golden boy. Would his family pay to keep an out-of-wedlock pregnancy secret?

Sure they would. Douglas would pay more today to keep his reputation pristine—and Wendy's murder forgotten.

Ross grabbed his cell phone from his pocket and punched in Zach's number. They were getting closer. Much closer.

Debra took a steadying breath, gripped the knife more tightly and roughly chopped the batch of cilantro on the cutting board in front of her. Leah's kitchen was bright and roomy and easy to cook in, but the friendly cozy atmosphere did nothing to calm her anxiety. She wasn't worried about how the meal would turn out. She'd been making her chicken enchilada recipe for years; it was one of Mia's favorites, so she could prepare it with her eyes closed.

Why was she so nervous? Because Jonah was coming. That was the reason why her hands kept shaking and why her palms were damp. She couldn't deny even to herself how much she admired Jonah. *Admired* him, she ordered herself. She was to admire him and nothing more.

But she could not stop the surge of hope at the sound of the front door opening or at the pleasant rumble of Jonah's baritone two rooms away.

"Mom! He's here!" Mia looked up from the kitchen table, where the girls had been working on crafts. With the clink of scissors hitting the scarred wooden tabletop and the scrape of the chairs against the floor, Mia and Olivia hopped up, their faces shining with delight.

"It's Jonah!" Both girls tromped through the kitchen and into the dining room, where china clinked on the shelves of the buffet as they skipped past.

The sounds of a real home, of a real family, made the cook's job even sweeter, Debra realized as she turned to the sink to rinse the blade. Although her back was turned to the doorway, she kept an ear out for the man's approach.

She was at the stove checking on the poaching filets of chicken when she heard the uneven strike of his gait on the oak floor. She turned at the sound of his approach. There he was, framed in the arched doorway. Her spirit uplifted at the sight of him. Of his smile. Of his respectful gaze. She loved the quiet, unspoken happiness that marked his rugged, handsome face.

"Flowers for the cook." He said the words simply.

The effect on her was anything but. Emotions tangled up inside her until she could not breathe or move.

He came closer and she could not stop a wish from rising up full-blown from her soul. She wished for the chance to spend more time with him. She wished for the chance for there to be more than friendship between them.

He slipped the bakery box he carried, which she only now noticed, onto the counter and strolled closer. In his other hand was a delicate china vase of fresh, pure white gardenias. "I hear these are your favorite."

"Y-yes." She sounded scratchy, but that was from the emotions untangling within her like a knot coming undone until there was one single truth. She was in danger of falling in love with him.

It wasn't sensible, it wasn't practical and it wasn't even wise. But that didn't stop the sweet affection from ebbing into every crack of her heart. "Gardenias are my favorite flower. Mia told you."

"She called me today and happened to mention it."

"Happened to? What else did she *happen* to mention?"

"Not much. She wanted to know how her furniture was coming along. And she mentioned you've been happier lately. You've been humming."

"Was I?" She certainly didn't remember doing it.

"I caught a bar or two while you were cooking. You have a good singing voice, I bet."

"I used to sing in the church choir long ago… You look shocked to hear that."

"By the way Mia is so determined to get you to church and save you, I thought you weren't a believer."

"I—I've had a lot of questions, I guess. I've taken a step back. It's more sensible."

"Faith is believing in what cannot be seen but

felt with the heart. *Sensible* has nothing to do with it." He leaned close and closer still until only the bouquet of flowers separated them.

Debra drew in a wobbly breath, feeling revealed in a way she never had before. Her heart was open again, vulnerable without a single shield to hide behind.

Panic thudded through her because if he could really see her and her flaws, her mistakes and insecurities, he might turn away from her. It was more frightening to think he might not retreat.

Terror tasted like copper on her tongue as she took a step back and hit the handle of the oven door. She had nowhere to escape. Jonah towered in front of her, all six feet of him. What did he see when he looked at her?

He set the flowers on the counter, his arm brushing her shoulder, bringing him close enough for her to smell the wood scent on his skin from his day's work. He stayed close, a whisper away, his dark eyes intent on hers, studying her as if he could see everything.

"Since you've had questions about faith, I've got to ask. What about love? You believe in that, right?"

"Sometimes. On a good day."

A slow smile showed his dimples. "Let's hope I can catch you on a good day."

She didn't know if he was talking about faith or love, but either way, she couldn't answer. He straightened away, giving her room to breathe and room to think. She was frozen in place. Although he'd put physical distance between them, he felt closer to her than ever before. Much closer than anyone had ever been. It was the sweetest feeling.

"Thank you for the flowers." There. She finally got the right words out and was rewarded by his smile. "I hope you like enchiladas, refried beans and nachos."

"What's not to like?" He leaned against the counter to study her with his serious, assessing gaze. "You do nothing but surprise me. About the time I think I've got you pegged, you do something that throws me off."

"And what exactly does that mean?"

"You have a high-powered career, yet you're a good mom, a kind lady and, judging by the delicious scent coming from the stove, a fantastic cook."

"I know you're simply being a gentleman, but I expect more honesty from a minister's son."

"You're not going to make this easy for me, are you?"

"Make what easy for you?"

He didn't say anything, just shook his head slowly from side to side. She would not give credence to the tiny twinkle of hope within her. It would not be sensible to let herself start to wish for the impossible.

Except, when she dared a glance at Jonah out of the corner of her eye, it now didn't seem impossible. Suddenly he launched away from the opposite counter to tower over her.

"Put me to work," he said.

So she did, sending him to open the cans of tomato sauce and tomato paste. She would describe cooking with him as companionable—nothing more would be sensible. But when she caught herself humming—twice—Debra had to realize there was more to it. Rolling up stuffed tortillas alongside Jonah made delight spiral through her. Being with him made her happier than she'd been in a long, long time.

Her feelings for him were far from practical. There was no longer any way to deny them. She topped the enchiladas with sauce and cheese, and as she put the casserole dish in the oven, she decided it would be best not to think about her feelings or her wishes for the future. She was going back to her life in a few days' time.

Maybe it was best just to enjoy this moment, this evening spent with this man.

Debra amazed him. Jonah did his best to hide his feelings and tried hard to concentrate on what Ben was saying to him as they were talking over the recent town news. But not even his iron will could blockade Debra from his thoughts, especially when he could hear the faint lilt of her voice as she chatted with Leah nearby.

When he shifted in the chair by the fireplace, she was at the edge of his vision. Talk about gorgeous. She wore a green sweater and slacks, a shade which brought out the chestnut tones in her brown hair. She remained at the edge of his conscious and he could not seem to shake her. If he looked away, he only listened more intently for the sound of her voice.

Face it man, you like her. Maybe *like* was too weak of a word. He feared that liking her wasn't the half of it. She was an easy woman to like—easy to get along with and truly fun when she relaxed a little. In the kitchen, she'd had him laughing over stories of ruined meals and cooking mistakes she'd learned when she'd first been on her own and he had to admit to a few of his own. When the meal was in the oven, they had joined the rest of the family in the living room, where the decorated tree glistened and winked in colorful splendor, and he missed that closeness with her all evening long.

For those few moments spent with her in the kitchen, he hadn't been racked with guilt, with what should-have-been, and memories of the friends he'd lost.

It was wrong, he knew, that he'd forgotten so easily. That he'd let anything distract him from his guilt and failures. The last few nights without sleep were catching up with him. Making him tired, making him weak. He gasped for breath and bounded onto his feet.

Ben watched him with a question on his face.

"I didn't realize how late it was getting." A feeble attempt, but it was all he could say as he made a beeline toward the front door. "Thanks for the hospitality. Debra, thanks for the fine meal."

"I'm glad you liked it." She rose from her chair, too, trailing after him to the entry. "I should have made more traditional holiday fare, but it's Mia's favorite."

"I think it'll be mine, too." He felt content, as if somewhere deep inside he believed there could be other evenings spent in her company, working side by side in the kitchen, sharing the little moments of laughter and closeness. He knew there couldn't be, but he wished for it anyway. "We have several days before you leave—"

It was the way she responded to his half-spoken suggestion that made every last word he'd been about to say fly out of his head. She watched him quietly with the smallest hint of emotion on her lovely face, and he could read it clearly: hope. Did she feel this, too?

He cleared his throat and fumbled for words. "I've got some time this week—"

He was cut off by the sound of boots coming in his direction. He'd forgotten that he and Debra weren't the only two people in the house.

Mia tromped into view, holding up a bulging holiday gift bag. "Jonah! You forgot the ornaments Olivia and I made. They're for your Christmas tree."

"Yeah, Jonah," Olivia chimed in, keeping close to her mom. "We worked really hard on them."

"Why, that's mighty thoughtful of you girls." He took the bag and peeked into it. "These are pretty decorations. Too fine for the likes of me. Now I guess I have to get a Christmas tree."

"You mean, you don't have one yet?" Mia slowly shook her head from side to side in complete disapproval. "Did you hear that, Mom? What are you going to do about that?"

"I don't know, kid." Debra drew her arm around her daughter, drawing her close, struggling to keep the corners of her mouth straight. "Jonah doesn't strike me as a humbug, but if he wants to be, I'm not sure there's anything I can do about it."

Her mirth was infectious. He couldn't resist teasing back. "I prefer my humbug existence. I'm not about to let two lovely ladies talk me out of it."

Ben added from across the room. "He's not as tough as he sounds. Debra, I say, go for it—date him."

To her credit, she blushed bright red. "Well, I don't know about that. When it comes to dating I'm very picky. What if I don't want to 'go for it' with a humbug?"

She had him there. Jonah snagged his coat from the closet by the door. "Maybe I'm not such a humbug."

She was still blushing.

He jammed one arm into the sleeve of his coat and then the other, and the red foil bag of decorations crinkled and rustled as if hinting at him, too. "Let's say I get a Christmas tree. I'm going to need some help with these fancy decorations."

Mia clasped her hands together and danced

in place, as if trying so hard to hold back her youthful enthusiasm. She struggled to sound grown-up and calm. "I'm sure we could help you with that."

"Not if you don't really want to," he couldn't help kidding her. "I can tell you really aren't thrilled at the notion."

She laughed. "Oh! You know I'm trying to get my mom to help you!"

"I'm fully aware of that." He took in the deeper shade of red staining Debra's lovely face and gave thanks for it. That gave him courage. "What do you say, Debra? Want to go Christmas tree shopping with me?"

"Oh, well, if it will help celebrate the season. I can't have you turning into a grinch."

It was what she didn't say that he heard so well. Somehow, he knew she felt as bashful as he did about these feelings. They were a lot alike, he realized. And he liked the idea of being with her—but there was one catch. He was afraid to be alone with her, afraid of where these feelings would take him. He had no right giving Debra the idea that he could be serious about her.

"I appreciate your concern," he said instead, "but what about Miss Mia? I might need her help, too. I am in serious danger of turning into a grinch."

"Wait!" Mia protested. "You two should, uh, go alone. So you can talk and stuff."

Debra wheeled toward her daughter, looking a little more than surprised. "What *and stuff* do you mean? What else would we do besides talk?"

"Uh…" Looking innocent, Mia rolled her eyes to the ceiling as if thinking up a reasonable answer.

Jonah figured he already knew. Miss Mia was looking for a husband for her mother. Debra hadn't realized that yet, but it looked as if she was starting to get the drift. He cleared his throat. "I can swing by the bed-and-breakfast and pick you up after work tomorrow."

Ben cut in. "It'll be dark by then. It might be best if you take off at noon and make an outing of it."

Leah rose to join her husband. "Yes, wouldn't that be nice? There's the tree farm just out of town where you can pick out your tree and they cut it down for you. We got ours there."

"It was real fun," Olivia added as an incentive.

Jonah was satisfied with that suggestion. He'd be able to spend time with Debra and it was a safe way to do it. His heart wasn't likely to get more involved if they kept it light. "There. That cinches it. I'll pick you girls up at noon, we'll grab a bite and head out to the farm."

"A bite?" Debra arched her brow.

When he'd first met her, he would have figured she was too sophisticated for a drive-through burger, but he knew her better now. "I've got one question for you. Do you have a weakness for French fries?"

"A terrible one." She said it without an ounce of shame. "Are you telling me that I'm going to have to blow my diet?"

"A diet? What do you need a diet for?" She was perfectly lovely. Then again, he was realizing exactly how biased he was when it came to Debra Watson.

"All right, my healthy nutritional food plan does not include fast food."

"Something tells me that you'll make an exception." He concentrated on zipping his coat. "I'll make it worth your while."

"Then how can I refuse?" She reached down to hold the placket for him, since he was zipping with the handicap of the bag.

He did his best not to notice the vanilla scent of her shampoo or the gentle curve of her face or the way his heart brimmed right over with tenderness for her. Yep, it was a good thing he was keeping things light.

Ben put his arm around his wife. "Debra. When you get to Jonah's eyesore of an apartment, make him show you the Purple Heart he keeps hidden in a drawer. I made the shadow box for him to display it in—but he's humble."

Did Ben have to mention that? Jonah yanked the door open to the frigid night. "On that note, adios. I'll see you two ladies tomorrow."

"We'll be ready!" Mia piped in. "Right, Mom?"

"Right." When Debra lay her hand on the open door, to close it after him, her gaze met his. "As one grinch to another, I think this will be good for both of us."

"You don't look like any grinch I've ever seen." He couldn't resist adding as he hesitated on the porch, with the freezing fog crisping around him. "You are far too lovely to be a grinch."

"You are wrong. Until lately, I hadn't realized how little I've been using my heart. What is the phrase? I think it's been two sizes too small, but I've decided to change that."

He didn't know how she could say such a thing, as good and kind and gentle as she was. Being with her brought him peace, made him feel like the man he used to be before the war. And he knew he was wrong for wanting to feel this way a little longer. It was wrong to want to stay in her presence and to feel whole. Instead of doing the right thing and moving away, he leaned closer and kissed her on her cheek.

"Tomorrow," he said with a wink. He turned on his heels, marched down the walkway and waited until he heard the door close in the stillness of the night before he looked behind him. It was her face he longed to see looking back at him through the window and she did not disappoint him. She blushed again, as if being embarrassed at being spotted, and let the curtains fall closed.

He was left with her image as he drove away, the vision of the kind of love he'd always figured he would have one day. That lost dream seemed to follow him home and haunted him right along with the nightmares throughout the long, merciless night.

The grandfather clock in the formal living room chimed the midnight hour. Douglas Matthews chugged back the tumbler of scotch and let the alcohol burn a fiery trail to the pit of his stomach. It felt like the pit of his soul.

It was starting to fall apart. All of it. The divorce papers he'd been served with stared up at him from the corner of the coffee table where he'd flung them. His vision was blurry from downing a good portion of the bottle of scotch, but he was still able to remember what his attorney had said.

She's got a good case, Doug. A doctor has confirmed her injuries are consistent with spousal abuse. You're lucky if she doesn't press charges.

"She wouldn't dare!" His words echoed with hate in the professionally decorated room. His showcase. What good was his image of a good Christian husband and father if his wife wasn't here with their boy, proof of his faith? How was he going to pull off his big Christmas special now?

He slammed the crystal tumbler onto the two-thousand-dollar coffee table. With surprise he realized the glass had come apart in his hand. When he shook his hand, crystal tinkled onto the tabletop and a tiny fissure of blood traced across his palm.

How about that? He didn't feel the pain. The scotch had numbed him, but not enough. A different kind of agony tore through him. Everything he'd done and he still didn't have the national show that he wanted. Didn't he deserve the best? Why shouldn't he be raking in all the fame and fortune he could? He was worth it. Didn't everyone understand that?

He thought of Lynda. She was probably floundering without him. She couldn't find her way out of a shoebox. She needed him. Let her have her little tantrum. Get it out of her system. She was probably regretting walking out on him and the advantageous lifestyle only he could give her.

Douglas sprang from the couch and paced the length of the room. Maybe everything wasn't falling apart. He could still save it.

The network deal was still in the works. Just because his agent was ready to dump him, didn't mean he had to take that kind of treatment. He'd turn the tables, get another agent, get his wife back and keep his image.

It all depended on his Christmas show. He had the feeling that was what it would take. He nodded, yes, he would go all out and do a family-values show. Everyone would see that he was still at the top and deserved more.

He stopped at the window and pulled back the drapes. The night was dark and stormy but not without hope. He was sure Lynda was trying to figure out a way to come back. She couldn't make it without him. He would try to show her what a good husband he was, ready to forgive her.

He went straight for the scotch bottle. A plan like this deserved a toast.

Chapter Ten

Mia pushed open the door and stuck her head into their rooms. "Mom! Jonah's pulling up in his big red truck!"

Debra kept her cell phone tucked against her ear and chin as she took one final glance in the beveled mirror. She was determined to look as casual about this outing with Jonah as she had decided to feel. "I have to go, Dad."

Her father sounded amused. "Sounds like you two are having a good time. But be sure and let Ben know that we'd like to see him and his family soon."

"I'll tell him." By the time she'd said goodbye and tucked her phone away, Mia already had her coat on and was frantically digging through her things.

"Have you seen my hat, Mom?"

"I have it, kid. It's here with mine."

"Whew." Mia swiped a shank of hair out of her eyes. "You look nice, Mom."

"Thanks, so do you, cutie." Debra grabbed Mia's coat along with her own. "Are you ready? We don't want to keep Jonah waiting."

"I'm glad you're wearing your hair down, Mom. It's really pretty." Mia tromped over to take her coat and snagged her hat off the edge of the bureau. "I'm glad you really like Jonah, too."

There it was again. They'd been too tired last night to talk about any serious issues and it wasn't as if they had a lot of time now. But as she tucked her wallet into her coat pocket and grabbed her keys from the dresser, she took time. "You know that Jonah can only be our friend, right?"

"But you really like him." Mia glanced up at her for confirmation.

Debra saw a flash of her daughter's dreams. Just a hint in the wide hopeful eyes and the way she bit her bottom lip, so vulnerable and idealistic in the same moment. "Are you hoping that Jonah and I will—" She hesitated, unable to say the words.

"Get married?" Mia supplied.

Oh, boy, Debra thought, here she was

worrying about liking Jonah too much and Mia was already planning the wedding. "Is that what you're hoping for? Is that why you wanted me and Jonah to go alone today? And why you invited him to dinner last night?"

"Well-l-l-l." Mia drew out the word, giving herself time to think. "You need a husband, Mom."

"Do I? That's news to me. What on earth has brought you to that conclusion?"

"You wouldn't have to work so hard if you had a husband." Mia shuffled out into the hall. "Plus, you wouldn't have to be alone with everything. Wouldn't that be nice? And—"

Extremely curious about what else her daughter had to say, she stepped into the hall, paying close attention as she locked the door. "And?" she prompted.

"And then maybe I could get a baby sister. I think that would be nice."

Sure it would, but Debra knew her child enough to know there was one more thing— and odds were that she could guess what it was. "You think that if we had a family like your cousin Olivia does that you wouldn't have to go away to school."

"Well-l-l-l, kind of. I was hoping that might work out. But mostly, as much as I hate school—and I really, really hate going away to school—I want a real family more. Don't you?"

Those words were like arrows to her heart. "I do, but you can't get your hopes up, kid. You know we're here for the rest of the week and then we go back home to Baltimore. Nothing can happen between me and Jonah. We're just friends, that's all."

"But I can tell you really like him. I mean, he's cool and you two like the same stuff."

"I know, but it's complicated. Love—the real kind that makes a marriage and a family happy—it just doesn't come along like snow falling from the sky. It's rare and I've never been able to find it." And, Debra didn't add, she didn't have a lot of confidence that the real thing would happen to her, as much as she wanted it to.

Mia took the stairs two at a time. "I keep telling you, Mom. You've got to believe in the power of prayer."

Debra froze at the top of the landing, watching her little girl float down the stairs. Once she'd been that innocent and naive, believing so easily in what could not be seen. Then she'd had to grow up very fast, and had vowed to not be so easily misled. That hadn't brought her peace or happiness and she wished, how she wished, she could grab hold of that innocence again to believe, truly believe in the power of what could not be seen. To trust in a power strong enough to change the winds of her life.

In the foyer below, the front door pushed open and there was Jonah in a haze of sunlight. She thought she felt a brush against her soul, like a touch from heaven. She wasn't usually so fanciful, but it did feel like more than hope, like believing again.

She watched Jonah find her on the landing and joy spread across his handsome face. Joy at seeing her changed his rugged features and made her hopes lift.

"Hey, there you are." He seemed to see only her. "Are you ready for an adventure?"

"Adventure?" Debra found herself gliding down the stairs, drawn to him. "In my limited experience, procuring a Christmas tree has always been a rather tame undertaking."

"Obviously you've never done this the right way."

Debra's boots took her straight to him. "Then I guess it's a good thing you came along."

"A very good thing." He held out his hand, palm up, and despite the wool of his glove, it was an intimate gesture and a protective one.

"Careful, snow's melting and the floor's wet and it's slicker outside. The freezing fog is making it tricky."

Yes, she was perfectly capable of noticing that, but it was nice of him to help out, since she wasn't noticing anything else but him. She wasn't sure what to think as she walked through the door he held for her and Mia, and followed her daughter down the walkway to the inn's cleared parking lot. Although the cement and blacktop had been carefully cleared, it was slick. Mia skated ahead, intentionally sliding and slipping toward Jonah's truck.

Maybe it was something in the air or maybe it was from spending so much time with Mia or, Debra realized, perhaps it was Jonah at her side that made the gray day feel like perfect weather. Whatever the reason, she was grateful for this day and this time spent with Mia…and, yes, Jonah.

The ride to Jonah's favorite drive-through was a short one. He pointed out his apartment in a newish complex as they drove past. He ordered cheeseburgers all around, milkshakes and big tubs of crinkle-cut French fries and golden onion rings. They ate in the warmth of the pickup, juggling ketchup packets and merry conversation. It was the best lunch Debra had

had in quite a while and she found herself laughing as freely as Mia, without worrying about her responsibilities and the messages accumulating on her voice mail from the office.

After they'd eaten way too many fries and the burgers were demolished, Jonah drove through town, pointing out landmarks like the gift shop Tony Conlon, the man who'd played Santa Claus, owned. Jonah added colorful stories of the town and the people he'd known all his life, while Debra and Mia sipped their chocolate-cherry milkshakes.

"Mom! Look!" Mia leaned across her to point at the bookstore. "There's a For Sale sign in the window."

"How could there be? I was just in there." Debra whipped around to catch a flash of a sign in the shop's front windows before it was out of sight.

There had been a sign in the window, but she hadn't been able to read what was on it. She remembered how happy the lady who owned the place—Pamela—had seemed running the place. "Could she really be selling?"

"I'm sure of it, Mom." Mia collapsed back against the seat. "I go to the Stanton School, you know, so my reading comprehension is very high."

Debra couldn't help it—she tilted her head back and laughed. She couldn't explain it. Maybe she'd finally heard herself reflected back in Mia's words. Normally, Debra would have been the first to agree and use it as the reason why Mia had to stay in school. But now, it was hysterical. She couldn't actually say why.

Jonah glanced at her. His dark eyes glittered with amusement. She supposed she was keeping him entertained. What had he said to her last night? *About the time I think I've got you pegged, you do something that throws me off.* He had that same look he'd had last night, one of amused puzzlement. Apparently she was surprising him again.

"Mom, you're laughing." Mia slowly shook her head from side to side as if she couldn't believe her mother's behavior, but she was giggling, too. "I mean, you're *really* laughing. For real. Like you're happy."

"I guess I am." Debra took a sip of milkshake and hoped the creamy thick iciness of the drink would help calm her. The happiness remained in her heart, like a little bubble of laughter. "How much does a bookstore like that cost?"

"Good question." Jonah finally spoke, his

brief gaze narrowing as he sized her up and then focused back on the road. He sat confidently with both hands loosely on the wheel, his air of capability unyielding. "Why? Are you interested?"

"Just wondering." That was the practical answer, of course. One didn't give up a comfortable life, a very well-paying job and family expectations to follow a less impressive dream, right? At least the Cunningham and Watson families did not. She sighed. She was so used to putting aside her dreams, it ought to be automatic after all these years. "The evening I was in the shop—"

"You mean, when we ran into one another?" Jonah glanced at her over the top of Mia's head and the puzzled look was gone from his face.

"Yes, that's the only time I've been in the shop. The owner mentioned her husband had recovered from a health crisis. Maybe that's why they're selling."

"Probably. They're at the right age to retire and enjoy themselves. Pamela has run that place day in and day out as long as I can remember."

"It's a lovely shop." A hint of longing sounded in her voice and she felt a little embarrassed. Surely Jonah did not want to hear about her complaints in life—she didn't want to hear them, either. Her life was what it had to be. As her mother had said long ago, "You keep the child and support her. It's your own fault you don't have a husband beside you, so you have to do the job of both. Cunninghams do not shirk their duties, especially not to family."

How long, Debra wondered, had she taken those words as law? As the only way to earn back her mother's love? To make up for her father's disappointment in her? To ease the guilt at Mia growing up without her father?

Now, remembering her talk with Jonah in Pamela's bookstore, she had to wonder if she'd taken her mother's words the wrong way. Maybe her mother had been speaking of her own life and regrets. Maybe Debra had spent her life doing what she thought her mother wanted, when that wasn't it at all.

The fog chose that moment to melt away like gray cotton candy being pulled apart. Wispy sheets of airy sugar melted before a cool blue sky. Streaks of sunshine cut like heaven's light on the endless rise and fall of the white land-scape. A billion sparkles in the snow winked and twinkled like the happiness inside her.

What a beautiful day. It had been a long time since she'd felt so much. Longer since she'd felt anything but the duty and responsibility she'd imposed on herself. She'd simply wanted her parents to love and forgive her. Most important of all, she'd been terrified of being a single mother and worked to provide security and comfort for her only child.

But she was starting to see there was more to life. More to loving. More to being a mother and a woman. She wrapped one arm around her daughter and drew her a little closer, as close as the seat belt would allow, and gave her a kiss on the forehead.

"Jonah, look! Is that the tree farm?"

"That's what the sign says." The amusement in his voice rumbled with a cozy feel.

It felt right somehow to be together with him. She liked—no, she loved—the way he was strong and quiet but gently good-humored. She watched him with new eyes over the top of Mia's flyaway hair and knew at week's end when she went back home she would miss him. Very much.

Jonah guided the truck off the road and into the parking lot marked by a low, split-rail fence. What impressed her most about him was that he seemed to know so many people, so she wasn't surprised when a man loading up a tree in the parking lot waved to him. The man's friendly smile and obvious regard for Jonah said everything. It was how everyone treated him. Her assessment of the man, unlike with Jeff, seemed to match everyone else's. Jonah was without a single doubt the kind of man who always did what was right and true. He had never let anyone down nor would he ever.

Maybe it was safe to admit just to herself that her heart was doing more than taking a little tumble for him.

By the time she'd unbuckled her seat belt and had opened her door, Jonah was there, offering his hand to help her down. She did not dare meet his gaze as she laid her woolen glove on his palm and stepped to the ground. It felt as if her heart kept going, falling all the way to the snowy down at her feet.

Behind her Mia was chattering away, thrilled by the crisp sunshine and scent of trees and the field stretching out ahead of them full of spruce and fir.

"We always get one from the lot by the church," Mia was explaining as Jonah shut the door. "Mom pays to have it delivered and we sometimes get to decorate it, but mostly we're too busy."

Jonah sounded amused as he hailed over a down-vested employee. "I've been too busy to get a tree lots of times."

"Yes, this year Mom ordered a tree without even seeing it and the decorator had it all done. I was away at school." Mia shook her head as if it was an obvious tragedy. "It's not tradition. Grandmother Millie always decorated her Christmas tree."

"Sure, now you quote tradition." Debra wrapped her arms around her daughter and gave her a quick squeeze.

"I know, I'm just saying—" Mia gave a good-natured huff. "Maybe sometimes tradition's good and sometimes something else is better."

"Maybe." Debra felt Jonah's gaze on her. He was quietly watching them with an inscrutable look—something more than approval and strangely like wistfulness. "How much room do you have for a tree in your apartment? Are we looking for something small? Medium? Huge?"

"Small. Definitely small." The sparkles in his eyes dazzled when he chuckled. "I can tell by the look of you two that I'm in trouble."

"You are a smart man, Jonah Fraser." Debra faced the approaching man with a name tag. "We're looking for a medium-sized spruce."

"Sure thing, ma'am. You want to head off to your left, those are our premium trees. I'll tag along and cut the one you choose."

"No need, Ted." Jonah held out his hand for the ax. "I see you're pretty busy. I'll do it myself."

"Seeing as how it's you, Jonah." The tree man handed over his ax. "My wife is sure happy with that new kitchen you and Ben did for her."

"Glad she's happy. See you later." Jonah hefted the tool, carrying it easily by the handle and keeping his stride short to stay at Debra's side. "I can see you're a take-charge kind of woman."

"You have a problem with that?"

"Not a chance. You've met my mother right? My sister? The men in my family learn quick how to hold our ground."

"I hope you don't mind Mia and I are picking out a tree for you. I agree with her. You need help."

"Don't we all." Jonah thought of what Mia had said to him in the church. "You look happier than when you first walked into the carpentry shop."

"I had a lot of worries when I first came, but they were for nothing. Ben is wonderful. It's that simple. He's so much like our brother Brandon, it feels as if I've known him forever."

"A good sign. The time here has been good for you. You look radiant."

"I do?" Surprise marked her face and she modestly waved his words away with a flip of her gloved hand. "This is the first time off I've had in forever. I think I took a week off when Mia was five to take her to the amusement parks in Florida. Mom and Dad tagged along with us, but other than that, I've been focused on providing for my girl."

"A worthy goal." He paused as Mia trotted ahead of them, looking at the trees. "You've done well with her."

"Thanks, I only hope she's happy. I would mortgage my future for that."

He didn't doubt it. "That's why the high-powered career. I get that. But what about those dreams you haven't talked about? Does the bookshop have anything to do with it?"

"Was I that obvious?"

"Your eyes give you away." She was so honest, he could read her more clearly than anyone he'd ever known. Sunlight burnished her, making her lustrous hair gleam with highlights and emphasizing her porcelain complexion.

He tore his gaze away because if he wasn't careful he was going to be the one who was starting to dream. "When Mia's father refused to marry you for her sake, I'm assuming he had no interest in financial support?"

"No, and I was too proud to force him. I took my mother's words to heart. I see now, thanks to you, that maybe there was another meaning to her statements, that she was speaking out of her own pain. But I loved her and I grew up. I graduated a few months later and I went straight to my family's publishing house."

"Some people in your position might have taken the easy path." He did his best not to look at her but kept his gaze on the sparkling snow directly ahead of his boots. "But I know you enough to guess that you've earned what you have in life."

"My position at the publishing house may have been expected, but no one works harder than I do, unless it's my brother Brandon." She shrugged, and her shadow riding before them on the snow shrugged, too.

"You still aren't telling me about your dreams."

"Some hurt too much, and the question is, how can something you've never had be so painful?"

"Wait one minute. Right there. That's proof of how strong the things are which you cannot see or touch." His shadow stretched ahead of him, taller and broader than her slim one. The image of them side by side together pulled at the dreams long buried and at a new one he wouldn't let himself see.

"I suppose you're right." She tucked a strand of hair beneath her cap, drawing his gaze.

Drawing his admiration. Time stood still as he felt the first strike of love in his heart.

Up ahead, Mia's voice cut through the stillness. "How about this one?"

When he found her up ahead standing in front of a fifteen-foot spruce, he figured she was being optimistic. "I'm not sure I could get that up the stairs and through the door. That's problem number one. Problem number two would be that my ceilings are ten feet high."

"Okay." Mia shielded her eyes against the sun with her hand to grin at him. "I'll find the perfect tree for you, don't you worry!"

Jonah chuckled. "She's determined, isn't she?"

"You're being a good sport, Jonah."

"She's great."

"Yes, she is." Debra leaned closer to him, so her voice wouldn't carry. "That lost dream you wanted to know about? It's nothing, nothing at all compared to the dream I got instead."

He was beginning to see that about dreams. "You got a good one there."

"I wouldn't trade her for the world."

Yeah, he was starting to feel that way about Debra. He folded her hand in his and, just so neither of them got the wrong idea, he explained. "The snow's deep here. I don't want you to slip."

Her smile told him that she understood what he couldn't say.

They walked together through the sun and snow with the fresh evergreen scent surrounding them, giving Mia all the time she needed to find the perfect tree.

Ross pulled to a stop outside the middle-class home and turned toward his passenger. Zach had been silent during the drive to this Richmond suburb. They'd both had a lot on their minds. Lynda Matthews had left her husband because he battered her. Wendy Kates had been with a man who battered her. Now they had to learn what Lynda knew before they could make their next move.

"He's got to be our man." Zach sounded sure.

"That's my hunch, too. I guess we're about to find out." He nodded toward the front door, which was already opening. A woman with light brown hair was peeking out at him.

Lynda Matthews. Ross pocketed his keys and led the way up the concrete walkway. As he got closer, he noticed the bruising on the woman's face. Greenish yellow around her eyes and across one cheekbone. Darker, newer bruises turning from deep black to purple on her jaw.

Sympathy filled him. "Thanks for agreeing to talk to us, Mrs. Matthews."

"Call me Lynda, please." As if uncertain, she backed up, pulling the door more widely open. "I want to do the right thing. Your sister, Trista, has been very k-kind to me. She's helping me when I need it."

"Trista will be glad to know that. I want to help you, Lynda. That's why Detective Fletcher and I are here. We want to make sure Douglas Matthews doesn't hurt you or any woman like this again. Will you answer our questions?"

"If I can. Come in." The woman looked withdrawn and she moved with care, as if she were nursing a cracked rib or two. "My son is with my mother, so we won't be interrupted. My dad is in the next room."

"He's welcome to join us if you'd feel safer." Ross waited for Zach to wipe his feet before coming inside. He closed the door, listening as Lynda talked nervously about Trista's call a few minutes ago. It had been a good decision to involve his sister.

After they'd sat down in the living room and refused offers of tea, they were able to get down to business. "My first question," he began, "is about Douglas's illegitimate daughter. Has he ever mentioned her?"

Lynda shook her head. "I had no idea. A daughter, you said? He never—" She swallowed hard. "He made me believe Logan was his only child. His first child. Then again, Douglas lied about a lot of things."

Zach took a turn. "Have you ever heard the name Wendy Kates?"

"Never."

"How about Barnaby Harcourt?" Ross asked next. "Did your husband ever meet with him or speak of him?"

"No." Lynda fidgeted and shifted position on the couch. She looked very nervous. "There was this one time I interrupted Douglas when he was on the phone. He was very angry, which had surprised me at the time. When he deals with most people, he uses his television voice. That's what I call it. The one that sounds so good and kind. He was furious and slammed down the phone. I noticed he had the checkbook out and he'd written Barnaby Harcourt as the payee. Douglas demanded to know what I s-saw. I didn't tell him the truth. I was afraid to. I remember stammering—I didn't know what to tell him—and he hit me. He told me never to interrupt him like that again. I never did."

Ross felt sickened by Matthews. He vowed to keep Lynda Matthews in his prayers. No woman deserved such treatment. He held back what he knew about Wendy Kates. Lynda had been luckier than other women who'd spent time with Douglas Matthews, he realized, and that was sad, too. "Has Douglas tried to contact you?"

"He's sent flowers, but I refused them. I know he's going to fight me for custody. He keeps calling, but I won't speak to him. I've asked Trista to file whatever papers we need to get a restraining order. I'm s-scared of Douglas, but I did the right thing ending my marriage. God didn't intend for a husband to be cruel to his wife."

"No, He didn't," Ross said as kindly as he could. "Thank you for your time, Lynda. If more questions come up, may I call you?"

"I'll help if I can."

Ross noticed the college and vocational-training catalogs on the end table. It was good that Lynda was making plans for a better life. He wished that for her.

At least he had some answers. Liam Matthews, Douglas's father, must have been paying Barnaby Harcourt off, and after Liam's death it sounded like Douglas had shelled out to keep his dirty deeds safely forgotten.

He waited until they were in the car heading back to the freeway before he asked Zach what he thought.

"I want the pleasure of cuffing him and hauling that rat to jail. What we don't have is hard evidence. It's all we're missing to nail him.

"We just have to be smart, that's all." Ross kept his eyes on the road, since the traffic was getting heavier. They had a long drive ahead of them and plenty of time to figure out a plan to force Douglas Matthews into showing his hand.

Chapter Eleven

Debra watched tiny snowflakes fly at the windshield of Jonah's truck and gave in to a cozy snuggle of contentment. She couldn't remember ever feeling this relaxed. Everything was just right. It had been, as Mia would say, the best day ever.

They'd decorated Jonah's tree while he'd found and replaced all the burned-out bulbs in his strings of Christmas lights. When they were done, the spruce looked festive with its flashing multi-colored glow and the paper snowflakes they'd added to the glittering stars and candy canes and silver and gold bells the girls had made.

She shot a glance over Mia's head to the man behind the wheel. Jonah was the reason the day had been special. All these years she'd felt alone, struggling to give Mia everything she deserved, working to please her family and to mend fences with her mother at a job she liked but didn't love. She'd been living a good life with so many comforts and yet she'd never known what was off, why she felt out of place and why true contentment had always eluded her.

She'd been missing a vital piece in her life, in her heart and in her soul. She'd forgotten how to dream.

"Oh! I know where we are!" Mia spoke up, bobbing on the seat to point up ahead. "We're near the mayor's mansion, right? Where we saw the tree-lighting ceremony? I wanted to see that street of lights. Can we? Please?"

"I don't mind. How about it, Deb?"

The way he said her name made emotions ball up in her throat. Emotions she had to try to keep reined in. "Sure, it's a lovely area of town."

"I like it, too. I always figured I'd live around here one day." He hung a right, nosing the truck down the frosty street that glowed under the influence of thousands of twinkle lights.

"Wow." Mia twisted against the seat belt to get a better view. "I want to live here, too. This is awesome."

Debra felt dazzled, as well. For as far as she

could see down the street, every home was tastefully decorated with lights and festive displays. It wasn't casually done. Great care and effort showed in the glowing candy canes marching up the walk to the front porch of the house on her right. Lit reindeer grazed on one lawn beneath perfectly blue icicle twinklers on the next house. Lights blazed like wonder.

Jonah parked against the curb. "Locals call this street Christmas Lane. It's even in the sales agreements so the people new to the street have to keep up the tradition."

"There's other people looking, too." Mia pointed out as she unbuckled her seat belt.

"The house at the end of the row collects donations for our church toy drive, so it's all for a good cause." Jonah cut the engine and pocketed his keys. "Want to take a walk?"

More than anything. By the time she'd opened her door, Jonah was already there. It felt right, it felt as if every missing piece were in place as she let him help her to the ground. She crunched through the frozen snow to the cleared sidewalks while Mia trailed after her. Crystalline perfect flakes whispered from sky to ground, a soft accent to the view. Upscale, roomy homes sat on wide lots with plenty of trees. It was like a street out of a storybook. She could see why Jonah said he'd always wanted to live here.

She recognized the cadence of Jonah's gait as he joined her on the sidewalk. Again, peace stirred through her like the breeze through the snow at his nearness. Maybe her heart was trying to tell her something.

"Nice, huh?" he asked.

"Very Christmassy. It's festive enough to put *me* in the spirit of the season."

"Excellent." His smile was slow and true.

His smile captured a little more of her heart.

Debra, Debra, Debra, she thought, *you're going to get hurt if you keep this up.* But did that stop her? No. Not from moving a hint closer to him. Not from letting the emotion she'd been holding back into her heart.

"Hey, Mom!" Mia was two houses ahead, pointing at one of the homes. "Look!"

It was a house out of her dreams. A modest brick Tudor was outlined by dripping white lights. Smaller twinkle lights framed a wide front porch and a bay window. The living room was visible behind the window glass and the room looked cozy from the soft glow of the impressive Christmas tree and a fire crackling in a brick fireplace. Debra didn't mean to be too nosy, but she couldn't help being drawn by the sight of handcrafted floor-to-ceiling bookcases full of books.

"Oh, that's the Lansbury's home."

The owners of the bookshop. That explained all the books. Did that mean the house would be going up for sale, too?

No, don't even begin to breathe life into that dream. She had to be sensible, although with Jonah at her side it was nearly impossible.

Another car pulled up to park. She steeled her spine and forced her boots forward down the walkway past the beautiful house to keep up with Mia, who was a few paces ahead studying every festive detail she could see.

Jonah kept pace with her. "What does your family do for Christmas?"

"When my mom was alive, she would make dinner on Christmas Eve for everyone. A formal occasion. We're talking the best china and silver, candlelight and our best clothes. We've tried to keep the tradition since. I'm not the same quality of cook, but my sisters-in-law and I do all right. After dessert, we head over to our church and attend services. Christmas Day is more relaxed with a traditional turkey dinner. How about your family?"

"We are way less formal." Jonah's baritone warmed as he spoke of his loved ones. "With my dad being a minister, my folks are as busy as can be this time of year. But ever since I was a little guy, we set aside time after the Christmas Eve service to watch *It's a Wonderful Life* and eat fudge."

"One of my favorites."

"The movie or the fudge?"

"Both." She liked how he chuckled warmly and how his voice was her favorite sound. The entire world was better when she was at his side. She adored everything about him and as she breathed in the fresh crisp air and felt the kiss of winter on her face, she realized she didn't just adore him. She loved him.

"Hey, Mom! Come see!" Mia was a house ahead, pointing at one of the front windows. "It's a nativity scene. I love it."

"Coming, kid." Debra tried to focus, tried to act as if nothing monumental had changed, but when Jonah tucked her hand in his much bigger one, it was impossible. As they walked side by side, it felt as if they belonged together. The empty, dark places in her heart filled with pure sweet love as promising as those twinkle lights. Glowing like hope, like wonder, on this cold winter's night.

Mia led the way up the front steps to the inn. Jonah heard her call out, as if from very far away although she was only a few yards ahead. "I'm freezing! I'm gonna go in!" Debra answered, but her words didn't register. Her loveliness did.

He couldn't remember a better afternoon. He couldn't have had better company. For the first time since he'd come home from Iraq, he felt at ease. Not even worship and prayer had been able to touch him like this.

Mostly, he realized, because he wouldn't let it.

On the top step, Debra turned to him, her complexion rosy from the cold and, he hoped, from happiness. "You've given us such a wonderful day, I think I should return the favor."

"I like that idea." He definitely loved the idea of seeing more of her. "What did you have in mind?"

"I have no idea. Maybe I'll just surprise you."

"Sounds good." Jonah cleared the emotion from his throat, but it stuck stubbornly as ice to his boots. "I've got a busy week meeting the needs of a very demanding client."

"Mia." She tilted a little to the left to glance through the windows flanking the front door to keep her daughter in her sight. "She is pretty excited about the new bedroom set."

"She seems pretty excited about everything."

"Where she gets the energy, I'll never know." Debra glimmered from happiness, her inner beauty striking him anew.

Jonah cleared his throat and stared hard at the toes of his boots. Today had been nothing more than borrowed time. He knew that. What he couldn't do was to start to believe he had a chance with her. No matter what he felt, she was nothing more than an undreamed dream.

He knew one thing for certain. He was glad just to be with her. "I know you haven't got a lot of time left and you're busy, but drop by the carpentry shop anytime. You will make my day."

"I notice how you didn't mention Mia."

"Hey, now, I didn't do that on purpose. I meant you, meaning you or both of you. I'm good either way."

She studied him, her gaze thoughtful. "Not a lot of men would say that about a woman with a teenaged daughter. Wait, I can't believe I said it like that. I've been actually avoiding that word."

"Teenager?"

"That's the one. It terrifies me, and not for the reasons you think."

"Oh, I don't know about that. I can see you pretty clearly. You're terrified because she's growing up and she'll be an adult soon. She's not a little girl anymore."

"You do understand me. Maybe it's because she's my only baby, but I want to treasure these years with her. I look ahead and I start counting the milestones. Mia's coming out. Getting her driver's license. Preparing her valedictorian speech from Stanton. Packing her off to Harvard." Her eyes silvered with emotional tears. "I don't have anyone else to focus all of my love on, I guess is the real problem. And I have to let go of her, send her off to school, just when I want to hold on a little more tightly to this time left with her."

"So if that's how you feel, what's the deal with this school she's going to?"

"It was my mother's wish. And if there is one thing I never want to do, it's to disappoint Millicent Cunningham Watson ever again, even if she's no longer on this earth."

"You don't think she'd understand?"

"I'm starting to hope that she would have." She corrected. "You dodge direct questions very nicely."

"Glad you noticed. I was in reconnaissance, so I'm at my best observing and listening."

"That's very annoying, I'll have you know."

That cracked him up. He couldn't help laughing, the sound echoing in the night. He could tell by the way she was smiling at him that she wasn't annoyed, not at all. Good to know.

"On that note, I'm retreating while the going's good. Good night, Debra." He took a step back. "I'll see you soon?"

"Maybe." The twinkle in her eyes said differently.

He took one last long look at the picture she made standing in the twinkle of the Christmas lights through the windows. Snow glistened like jewels in her hair and lay like diamonds at her feet. She was what he wanted his future to be, if he had the right to one.

He was alive, when others were not, to walk down the sidewalk and he could feel the burn of icy cold on his face. He was alive to love and work and wish, and the guilt of it drew the laughter from his spirit and the love from his heart. If he could have one prayer answered on this cold winter's night it would be to change the unchangeable, so that he would be worthy of loving her.

Debra watched Jonah drive away in the worsening storm as she closed the door. Possibilities whispered at the back of her mind, hopes that she was almost able to give voice to.

"He's nice, isn't he, Mom?"

Mia. Debra turned to see her daughter collapsed into the chair near the fire. "I don't believe it, kid. You actually look worn out."

"I'm bushed." Mia propped her suede boots on the hearth. "Jonah liked his tree, didn't he?"

"Absolutely. He said it was the prettiest one he'd had in years."

"Yeah, but why hasn't he had a tree before? I get that he goes home to his mom's and stuff, but we have our tree even though we celebrate Christmas at Grandfather's house." Mia watched the fire. "Jonah seems sad a lot."

"I noticed that, too." Debra drew an ottoman close and slid onto it.

"I was snooping—I know I wasn't supposed to—but I couldn't help it. It wasn't private or anything, but I happened to notice there was a framed picture facedown on the little table in the corner, the one hidden behind the couch?"

"The couch we moved to accommodate the enormous tree?" Debra nodded. "You shouldn't have been snooping, kiddo."

"I said I knew that, but, well, I couldn't help it. I mean, Jonah had a ton of other pictures on the wall framed for everyone to see. But this one—I thought maybe it had fallen over, at least, that's what I told myself. It was a picture of a bunch of military guys—and Jonah—with guns."

"You heard Ben say that Jonah was a marine."

"Do you think he was in the war?"

"Yes, I do."

Mia gave that some thought. The fire crackled and a distant clinking and clanging came from the direction of the kitchen. Finally, she spoke again. "Do you think he got hurt? That's why he limps?"

"Yes." Jonah had been amused when she'd pointed out how he was far from forthcoming about his problems. He'd been a recon marine, which was Special Forces. She didn't know much when it came to the military, but she'd read enough to know that. "Now, let's get upstairs. I think we have just enough time to get in a call to Aunt Lydia before it's too late."

Mia uncrossed her ankles and dragged herself upright. "But first, there's one more thing."

"Only one more? I know you, cutie, and it's never just one more thing."

Mia tossed her hair over her shoulder. "Okay, there's at least two things. I really liked that

Christmas-light street we walked down. I think you should quit your job and I should quit the Stanton School—"

"I see where this is going."

"—and you could buy the bookstore and a house on that street where we could live happily ever after. You could even get married. I wouldn't mind a baby sister, you know."

"I've heard something like this before. You have high hopes, don't you, kid?"

"Yep, 'cause I believe in the power of prayer. You should, too."

"I almost think I can."

"Really? My work is almost done." Mia climbed to her feet. "Hasn't this been the most incredible trip?"

"It has been a good holiday."

"Not only did we get a whole new family to love, but the impossible happened, Mom." There Mia went, being a touch dramatic again, and also as sweet as pie. "You actually started liking a guy. *That's* a miracle."

Had it been that obvious? Debra unzipped her coat and hurried up the stairs after her daughter. She was so happy, she felt as if she could float up the steps like a helium balloon. Mia was right. Her life was changing. Her heart was changing, too. She'd come to Chestnut

Grove expecting the worst. What she found was the best—and Jonah. Who knew where this would lead her next?

Well, God did. Why that thought reassured her, she couldn't say, but she was glad for it as she heard Mia's voice through the door, already chatting away to her aunt. Full of hope for the future, Debra opened the door and stepped inside.

Maybe it was the drive back home through the icy streets and the walk through the subzero temperatures from the parking lot to his front door, but reality was starting to edge in. Jonah turned the bolt and stepped through the threshold. He couldn't stop thinking over the day and the woman he'd spent it with. The image of her with the snow falling all around her and sticking to the dark mane of her hair made him ache with disappointment too strong to stomach.

You don't deserve her, man.

He dropped his keys and cell phone on the table behind the couch and noticed the face-up picture, in a simple black frame he'd made himself. The snapshot showed a company of force recon marines in base camp. He studied the grinning faces of his buddies in full gear. They'd been preparing for a mission. Their spirits had been high, but it had been early in the war. The gritty dust of the Iraqi desert hung in the air. After three years he could still taste it on his tongue and feel the film of it on his skin.

For one brief instant he was back in that long-ago moment. He could feel the jolly camaraderie. One thing recon marines had was the constitution to handle pressure. They'd been packing their gear and giving each other a hard time when Austin had pulled out his camera. They'd been men in their prime, well-trained and they knew it, and that confidence hung in the air like the dust. It was what he remembered most now. That optimistic, confident moment as he crowded in next to Benton, his best buddy, whom he'd failed.

His grief and guilt was so deep it was a sinkhole taking him down. There was no escape. He hung his head, lost. So lost.

He didn't know how long he stood in the dark, but the shrill jingle of his phone brought him back. He snatched up the cordless receiver, still half in the past. "'Lo?"

"Jonah." His mom's voice, cheerful and loving and alive with goodness.

It made him feel all the places within his soul that weren't. He cleared his throat, but the emotion was still there, sticking like peanut butter.

Mom chattered on, unaware. "I've been swamped with everything, but the Christmas Eve program is going to be inspiring this year, as always. I've been meaning to drop by and check on my boy."

"I haven't been a boy in a long time," he told her, as he often did.

"I know, but you're my son." Love shone in her voice with unyielding confidence in him. "You didn't return my calls. I've left *two* messages."

"I know, I got 'em." He rubbed at his forehead. A headache was building. "You need anything? I'm here to help."

"I can always count on you."

Jonah hung his head again, her words hitting him like a cluster bomb. His hand shook as he turned the picture of his company face down.

Mom, bless her, kept talking. "Now that we've got that new DVD player, I wanted to upgrade our Christmas movie because we've worn out our VCR tape. I can't seem to make it to the video store, and when I ran errands and actually remembered to stop, they were out of stock. I'm enlisting you to run over to the bookshop to see if they have a copy."

"It's an easy mission."

"What a relief. I've got more problems I need help with." Mom didn't sound overburdened or stressed, Jonah realized, but unusually chipper, even for her. "Especially one very upsetting one."

"I can take care of it. What's wrong?"

"My son has been seen all around town with a certain lovely young woman and he has told me nothing about it. Can you imagine such a thing?"

Uh-oh. That smile in Mom's voice should have been a big, neon clue, but he'd missed it. Time to do damage control. "I didn't tell you about Debra because there's nothing newsworthy to tell."

"You two aren't dating?"

"What made you think we were? You were just hoping for it." He wished he could hope for it, too. "Before you get all excited and start making plans—

"What kind of plans do you mean?"

How could the woman sound so innocent? Jonah wondered. "You know what I mean. Debra lives in another state."

"Maryland. It's only a few hours away. And she's wonderful. I was just talking with Leah Cavanaugh and she loves her."

Of course she does, Jonah thought as he

crossed to the couch and dropped onto it. Who wouldn't love Debra? He couldn't imagine it, maybe because he was trying to keep away from using that word himself. Time for a diversionary tactic. "Hey, how's the pageant prep coming along?"

But his mom was a sharp tack. "Nice try, big guy, but I'm not satisfied yet. My sources say you've been seen at the diner, at the drive-through, at the tree lot and walking down Christmas Lane with Debra and her daughter. That doesn't sound casual to me."

Forget diversionary tactics. His mom should run the CIA. "How do you manage to gather so much intel?"

Humor warmed her voice. "Oh, I have my sources. You know how it is. My secret informants. You haven't answered my question."

"Yep, and on purpose, too." Jonah leaned forward and plugged in the lights. The bulbs on the tree flashed on, reminding him of Debra and how happy he'd felt when she was here with her daughter, filling his apartment with life and laughter, decorating the tree.

He had to be realistic where Debra was concerned. "I know you keep hoping I'll settle down."

"Hoping? I'm praying as hard as I can. You

haven't dated since you came back from the war. There are so many nice, available young women at our church, and nothing. Not one rumor has floated back to me about one single date. And then, suddenly, this. You know how that gets my hopes up for you. I want you to be happy, Jonah. I know what you went through over there and you deserve happiness."

Happiness? That was the last thing he could be worthy of. The real killer was that he couldn't tell his mom why. He'd never told anyone here the truth. He pressed the heel of his hand against his forehead, where his headache was building. "I'm content enough, Mom. You don't need to worry about me."

"Not worry about you? Why, it's all I do. I see more than you think I do."

His mother's love was a given, and he could hear it now in her voice, erasing the miles between them but not the agony in his soul. He had to be clear—to his mom and to himself. "Debra and I are friends. That's all. That's all we can be."

"You never know. Things have a way of changing. I hear she's staying for Christmas Eve services. You could invite Ben and his family—all of his family—to sit with us."

Jonah stared at the colorful flash of lights on

the tree. Bright. Dark. Bright. Dark. A ball of emotion felt glued to the back of his Adam's apple. He cleared his throat again. "Leave it alone, Mom, please."

"You know I'm here for you. I'm eight minutes away. I can make it in six if you really want me to."

Love, only love in those words. Agony tore through him, because he didn't deserve it, he wasn't worth it and, even knowing this, he ached for peace and a way to heal the impossible—all of that was hopeless. There would be no peace and no healing for him.

"No, Mom." The words felt ripped from his throat. "Thanks. I love you for it, but no."

"All right, I'll stop pushing. But I'm going to send your dad over to check on you."

"Not tonight, Mom. I've had a long day. I'm just tired." He rubbed at his temples.

"Tomorrow, then. I love you no matter what, Jonah."

More wounds to his soul. She didn't know what she was really saying. He thought of the lives ended and families that were destroyed because of it—because of his failure—and he lost strength completely. Not even faith could comfort him or touch him.

"Good night, Mom. I'll pick up the movie."

He heard his mom saying goodbye. He clicked off and let the phone drop from his fingers onto the couch.

The lights kept flashing. Dark. Bright. Dark. Like the flash of rockets across the Iraqi night sky, the flash of bright light and color seized him and yanked him back into memory. Into the scouring sand against his face as he lay stretched out, belly down in his ranger grave with the comfort of his M16, locked and loaded and ready to go. Ready to protect and defend.

Jonah felt the first concussion of the migraine and leaned forward to pull the plug on the Christmas lights. The lights died; darkness reigned. He knew these memories, newly triggered, would haunt him in his dreams tonight, where he would fight with all his strength to change the outcome and save lives; things that not even God could do.

It was going to be a long night.

Chapter Twelve

Douglas slammed shut the front door so hard, it rang like a bullet crack in the quiet house. Pain shot through his head—he'd had too much fun last night. It wasn't fair. He hadn't even dressed for the day yet and already it sucked. For the second time this week, he'd been served legal papers. First the divorce documents and now the restraining order.

Rage roared through him as he tore the envelope and hurled it at the wall. He felt like hitting something, but his head hurt too much. He needed a couple of aspirin and plenty of coffee first. Then he'd deal with Lynda.

He grabbed the carafe of coffee from the station and poured a big cup. Who did she think she was, refusing his flowers? Blocking his phone calls and betraying him like this? She was his wife. She had no right denying him anything. A restraining order! No paper was going to tell him what to do with his own wife! He stormed through the house to the kitchen. This was all her fault. If she didn't make him so mad, he wouldn't lose his temper with her.

He angrily jabbed the carafe back on the burner. The morning news droned on the television in the family room. The words *Tiny Blessings* caught his attention. He carried his cup around the island so he could see the TV. A man with dark hair and a bit of stubble filled the screen. It was that investigator. Ross Van Zandt.

"—a major development in the adoption scandals has been discovered at the Tiny Blessings offices. A prominent Chestnut Grove family is involved. We will be handing over important evidence to the police after the holiday—"

What evidence? The cup slipped from Douglas's hand and crashed to the tile. Hot coffee splashed across his slippers. He was so angry the image on the plasma screen blurred. That nosy private eye! They must have found some documentation about Wendy. Douglas felt sure of it. He started to tremble. The pain in his skull ratcheted up a notch.

If the truth came out, he'd be ruined. Everything he'd worked for. All his plans. It would be over. He'd lose his national show, his local show, his cars, his house—everything. Fury roared through him like hot lava.

No woman was going to destroy his chances. He went in search of the aspirin bottle, banging through kitchen cabinets as he went. He had to get rid of this headache so he could work out a plan.

He could fix this. It wasn't too late. He refused to fail. He would make sure there was no evidence. And without evidence that private eye and the cops couldn't link him to Wendy. He'd be free. He'd have everything he wanted.

Douglas grabbed the bottle of aspirin from the cabinet above the stove and popped two onto his palm. He would outsmart Ross Van Zandt tonight. No scruffy private eye was going to be the downfall of The Douglas Matthews.

Possibilities. Debra felt the lightness of it as she impulsively pulled her SUV into an empty parking spot—a miraculous event in itself—in front of the little bookshop. She checked the clock—she had a few moments to spare before delivering the surprise lunch basket to Jonah, which she had packed and ready to go on the seat beside her.

As she buttoned up and stepped out into the glittering winter day, something Mia had said came back to her. Two busy days had passed by in a pleasant blur packed with Christmas shopping and baking with Leah. But even so, Debra could still hear her daughter's words as clearly as they'd been spoken on the wonderful day spent with Jonah. *You could buy the bookstore and a house on that street where we could live happily ever after. You could even get married. I wouldn't mind a baby sister, you know.*

I wouldn't mind those things either, Debra thought. Those things were, in fact, the most precious dreams she could imagine. So precious she could only let herself hope for them a little. To shield herself from getting hurt, she realized as she picked her way through the snow and onto the sidewalk. Isn't that how she'd been living her life ever since she'd taken Jeff's abandonment and her mother's criticism so hard?

A lightbulb moment. She would give that some thought later, she decided as she held open the front door for a young mother pushing a baby stroller, allowing herself to study the adorable baby boy with hope. There was so much she wanted for her life and for Mia's and that hope buoyed her as she stepped into the shop and looked at it with new eyes.

It really was perfect. She took in the luster of the polished, beautifully crafted bookshelves stretching in neat rows, the children's book section in the corner so colorful and inviting. She felt those buried dreams fill with optimism—and, yes, with faith.

"Oh, welcome back," Pamela greeted from behind the register as she bagged up a customer's purchase. "Please let me know if you need any help."

"I do, when you get a chance."

"Be right with you."

Debra stayed close by but couldn't resist browsing while the shop owner finished ringing up her sale. Pamela chatted away, she seemed to know everyone by their first names and many details about their lives. Debra supposed it would be a nice thing, not just to own a bookstore but to know the people who were regular customers. It was friendlier, somehow, a business with heart.

Could I really make a change like this? Debra wondered as she noticed a small rack of movies set out in the holiday section. Could she quit her job and give up a very comfortable living for something less secure but, oh, so much more fulfilling?

She spotted a single copy of *It's a Wonderful Life* and plucked it out of the little wire holder. This was the movie Jonah said was a holiday tradition for his family. She hadn't watched it in years. The story had always touched her, a man who always worked hard to do the right thing for his family and for others, deferring his own dreams.

"Whew, we have a lot of last-minute shoppers." Pamela broke into her thoughts. "What can I do for you?"

Her heart kicked into a staccato beat, and she felt as if she were standing on the edge of a bridge, looking down, afraid. She realized how very much she wanted this dream. "I was wondering about the For Sale sign in the window. How much does a business like this cost?"

"It's not a business, but more." Pamela's kind eyes silvered with emotion. "I'm considering an offer right now, but I'm not happy with it. Are you interested in buying my store?"

"I don't know, truthfully. I'm just asking on impulse." A serious impulse. "I was hoping you could give me a ballpark figure. Are you looking for a cash offer? Or would you rather sell and carry the contract for tax reasons?"

"I'd like to carry the contract." Pamela

blinked hard to hold back her emotions. "My husband and I built this business side by side. I don't want to sell the place to someone who wants the property and not the bookstore."

The other offer, Debra imagined. "I've always wanted to own a shop like this. Full of love and care and personal touches."

"Yes, that's exactly the kind of offer I'm looking for." Pamela lifted her glasses to swipe at her eyes. "I'm sorry, you must excuse me. As much as I'm looking forward to retirement with my dear husband, it means letting go of this place I've also loved so many years."

"Believe me, I understand." Debra saw a lifetime's work in this place. A lifetime of helping friends, not customers. Of helping others find just the right gift or book to inspire them. She saw her dearest dream deferred, given up for her daughter's sake. Was it something that she could have now, for Mia's sake, too?

"I hear your family are book people." Pamela pulled a tissue from her cardigan sweater's pocket. "Christian publishers?"

"Yes. You carry our books."

"Then make me an offer, if you'd like. I can give you my attorney's card?"

"Please." Debra was touched by the woman's

friendliness and followed her to the front desk. "I'd like to get this, too."

"Oh, you got our last copy." Pamela stepped behind the desk to work the register. "A last-minute Christmas gift?"

"Yes, it is." Debra fished her credit card out of her purse and slid it onto the counter. "The perfect gift, too, I think."

"Oh, isn't that a good feeling? To give someone what you know is just right for them." Pamela swiped the card and handed it back. "Can I ask who it's for?"

"Jonah Fraser." Debra wasn't surprised when Pamela smiled as if she knew the man well.

"Such a nice one, that Jonah. He'll appreciate this." Pamela added a folded sheet of wrapping paper into the bag with the book. "I noticed you two together when you were in last. You make a nice couple."

"Oh, we're not—" Debra felt her face heat and knew she was blushing. "We're just—"

"Oh, I know how it is." Pamela's eyes twinkled with understanding as she handed over the bag and a pen. "Please sign here and you're ready to go."

"Thank you." Her signature was a little shaky on the credit slip, but other than that, she felt good, as if the pieces of her life were starting to fall into the right place. As if the past was no longer hurting her.

After tucking the gift out of sight, she drove the few blocks to the carpentry shop. She felt so light and free, that she sent a tentative prayer heavenward. *Please, let this dream come true.*

She pulled into the parking lot and saw the window where she'd first set eyes on Jonah and added one more request. *Please, let the bigger dream for him come true, too.*

A peace washed over her with such power she knew without a doubt that she'd been heard.

The crack of rifles and the burst of machine-gun fire peppered the desert night. Jonah froze and knelt as the missile traced overhead. In the dark of the moon his team waited as tooth-rattling explosions from the marine artillery hit like powerful blasts of thunder. The earth quaked beneath his boots hard enough to make his bones hurt, but he didn't let the discomfort register. His attention was on the field ahead, a deceptive stretch of dried mudflats and shadowed patches of dried grass and stunted palms that looked silent and vacant.

He knew better. Just as he knew the nearly imperceptible pad behind him was his team member approaching like a shadow in the dark.

Benton knelt beside him, weapon ready, watching, too. They were always watching. Their search and rescue mission had turned into something tougher: the battle was coming their way. No explosives boys to clear the way. They had to move fast. They were running blind. He didn't like it, but it wasn't his call. He felt the telltale sharp increase of air pressure and called out, betraying his position. "Incoming!"

There was no time to do more than duck before the mortar hit. There was the boom as it struck. The blast of black smoke blotted out everything. It rained rock and sand. Adrenaline kicked through his veins as he felt every hair on his arms shiver and his teeth went numb. Just for a heartbeat. Then the next bang of mortar.

In the dark ahead, Jonah caught the sign from his XO. Their commanding officer was giving the go-ahead. He'd made it a meter into the field and held his position, ready to cover them. The whiz in the sky above warned of an incoming artillery shell, but he was already moving forward. With every tense step, he listened for any enemy movement in the bush and the near-silent pad of Benton at his side.

Mortar exploded closer, cratering the earth, blasting them with rock fragments. Burning

*sensations bit his left side. His mind told him
he was hit, but he ignored it. He fought to stay
on his feet. He heard the click, but realized it a
second too late. One horrible second too late.
Land mine, his brain rationalized, knowing it
was Benton who'd triggered it. Then the white
heat of light, the percussion blast and horror—*

"Jonah?"

He heard his name, but the dream claimed
him, holding him captive in time with death
and brokenness all around him and Benton—

No, it can't be true, his mind thought even as
he knew Benton was gone. His best buddy
since boot, his brother-in-arms.

"Jonah?"

It was Debra's voice pulling out of the nightmare of war, of the failures he could not endure.
Her voice guided him out of his shadows of
grief and into the light of day. When his eyes
opened, he found himself in the shop sitting up
in the corner. The first thing he saw was the
overwhelming love for him in her eyes.

Love. Unmistakable and real. She'd knelt
onto the cement floor in her upscale jeans and
the soft pink color of her sweater made her look
as innocent and as sweet as a rose. Her fingertips brushed at the hair falling into his eyes.
"Are you all right? Is there something I can do?"

"No." He realized he must have drifted off. He felt groggy and nauseous. Looking around he realized he was holding the plans for Mia's desk in his hands. He'd taken a break before starting on the next piece of furniture, now that the bed was finished, and that was the last thing he remembered.

"You were dreaming, Jonah. It looked like a terrible nightmare."

He was too shaky to stand so he inched away from her and swiped his hand through his hair, undoing what she'd done. He was too embarrassed, ashamed and dull with grief to answer her. He needed fresh air. He needed to feel the icy winter's wind against his face. He hated the sticky feel of failure and of regret big enough to land a jet on.

He stumbled to his nerveless feet. Disgrace. Dishonor. Both weighed on his heart. The shrapnel had struck more than flesh and bone. It was still wedged in his soul.

"Jonah?" She was coming after him.

He threw open the back door, breathed in the cold air and let the snow numb him until he could feel nothing—no guilt, no grief, no shame. Until he could no longer hear the silence that came after the rocks finished falling with no survivors directly around him. Until he could no longer remember the vibration of another mortar strike and the rat-tat-tat of a firefight across the dry riverbed.

"Jonah?" She was behind him. Her hand settled on his shoulder.

He squeezed his eyes tightly shut, but he could not shut out the comfort of her touch or the peace she threatened to bring him. The love and life and future he wanted so much with her tormented him. He would give anything for the chance.

But it was a chance he did not, could not, deserve. He saw the faces of the dead—his own team members, his best friend. His heart broke all over again.

"Jonah, you're hurting so much. Let me help you."

Her soothing touch and her concerned words burned through his pain. He tensed every muscle and made everything within him as cold and still as steel, trying to resist the need to give in to the comfort she offered.

He could feel the longing for peace tempt him into shrugging off this shame, in silencing these feelings of dishonor and guilt and to go on living anyway. But he was a man of honor, a marine with a soul-deep moral code and he could not turn his back on the past. He could not forget the men he'd fought beside any more

than he could stop time and trade their lives—
Benton's life—for his own.

"There's nothing you can do," he bit out. It
was only the truth. No one could save him from
this. No one. "Just leave it alone, Debra."

"I heard a little bit." Her voice trembled.
"You were murmuring in your sleep—"

"I shouldn't have drifted off, but I was tired.
Last night—" He stopped midsentence. He
could not talk about last night and the dreams.
Of Benton dying over and over again. Every
time he closed his eyes.

"You must have dreams like this every
night." Debra didn't give up or move away, but
lay her other hand on the flat of his back. "No
wonder you're tired. Whatever happened, it's
obviously a heavy burden to carry."

"You have no idea what went on. What I've
done." His throat choked on the words, making
them impossible to say. He did not have the
strength, the courage or the right.

"You are a strong, noble man with a big
heart." Debra spoke quietly but with absolute
unwavering confidence. "What could you have
done but your best?"

"You don't understand. You can't understand."

"Because I'm a woman? A woman who's
never been in combat? I have a heart, Jonah. I

can sympathize. I've read enough to understand. A soldier can be haunted later by what he had to do on the battlefield. The mind waits to process what happened until you are out of danger. Maybe if you talked about it—"

"No." He tore away from her touch. "I can't do that. I won't."

It was plain to see how deeply he was hurting. Perhaps he just needed to know he was safe. She took a step closer, lay her hand on his and gazed into his shadowed eyes. "You can trust me with your truth. I promise to understand."

"You can't understand. You think—" He grimaced, the image of perfect agony. "This isn't something I can talk about."

She felt his muscles tighten like iron beneath her fingertips. He radiated the kind of pain that she'd never known. It was a risk to tell him how she felt, but he needed her. She could not let him hurt like this alone. Her heart filled with the most tender, unconditional love for him. "I—I care about you so much, Jonah. Please, let me help you."

"I said no." He shoved away, breaking the moment, rejecting her comfort and, worst of all, putting the space of the shop between them. The distance seemed cavernous as he faced her

but it could not diminish his pure male fury—
not frightening, no, never that—but he looked
every inch the tough, steadfast and hurting warrior he was.

The man she loved. Not a little, not a lot, but
more than she could measure or describe or
put limits on. Love for him filled every crack
and fissure within her heart and spirit. A love
that nothing could diminish.

Not even his rejection. He needed her now
more than ever. Her love, her understanding, all
the heart she had to give. "Jonah, please I—"

"You don't know what you're asking," he bit
out, interrupting her harshly. His hands were
fisted. His entire body tensed with coiled self-
control. Only his eyes gave him away. His grief
looked as powerful as a black hole where no
light, no life, could escape. "I need you to
leave."

His words were like bullets to her exposed,
undefended heart. She took a step back and froze,
reeling under his hard words. That can't be right.
That wasn't the Jonah she'd come to know.
"You're hurting, but I'm here for you. I truly am."

"I don't need you, Debra. I don't need this."

Shock washed over her. She felt her heart
beat, air rushed into her lungs and tears burned
behind her eyes as his words sunk in. As his

intent sank in. He may be hurting deeply, but that wasn't why he was pushing her away.

"But I thought you felt—" The words died on her tongue as he shook his head no, as if he knew what she was going to say. He was already answering her.

"No," he said tersely. "I have been fighting how I feel for you. I have no right. I have n-nothing to offer you."

His eyes were an apology, but his words may as well have been mortar shells falling. Debra lay a hand over her heart, feeling the devastation of her dreams. The rubble of her hopes.

I have nothing to offer you. His words echoed in her mind. How could she have been so off track? Here she'd been starting to picture her life with Jonah in it—as her husband. And he wasn't looking beyond the moment. Maybe he couldn't. He was clearly in terrible pain.

"I'll just be going, then. I—I'll have Ben bring Mia by t-tomorrow to see the finished bed. It—it's lovely, by the way." Embarrassed and knowing she'd made a terrible mistake, she retreated to the picnic basket she'd left near the door. The wooden handle felt hard when she gripped it. She wished the shields around her heart could be as hard as wood, but her defenses were down, as they always had been around Jonah. He had the straight shot to her heart. Nothing could change that.

"Goodbye, Debra." He sounded gruff, but it was his sadness she felt in the air between them.

"Goodbye, Jonah."

She forced her chin up and held it together until the door clicked shut behind her. It had to be the snow striking cold against her face because she would not allow it to be tears.

Chapter Thirteen

"I'm glad you're staying for the Christmas Eve program tonight," Ben said as he joined Debra in front of the Cavanaugh's Christmas tree. "It means a lot to Olivia that her Aunt Debra gets to watch her sing."

"It means a lot to me, too. She's such a sweetheart. It was nice of Leah to take Mia with her and Olivia tonight. She's very excited about the Christmas Eve program." Debra slid the final gift she'd brought for the family under the tree and folded up the super-sized shopping bag thoughtfully.

Ben studied the rather sizable contribution she'd made to the presents already beneath the tree. "I see you've already started spoiling your new niece and nephew."

"It's a job I take seriously." With the whirlwind of preparing for the holiday and keeping up with Mia and silently grieving Jonah's lack of love for her, she hadn't found the right time to talk with Ben alone the last few days. Now she had the opportunity. "When I first heard about you, I didn't know if I could get past my initial feelings. I loved Mom. I used to think she could do no wrong. That she was the greatest woman I'd ever known."

"I didn't mean to cause you any hurt."

"You didn't. It's been me. All me. I didn't know how to process this. How to make sense of it. Mia said that those documents were found because of God's intervention. That because we'd lost Mom, we were given new family to love. I didn't believe her."

He winced. "I had hoped that time would change that."

"It doesn't need to. I only had to spend a little time with you to feel as if I'd always known you. You are a lot like our brother, Brandon. You have Mom's eyes, just like the rest of us have. I'm glad I've had this chance to stay and know you better. To see that Mia was right."

Ben's throat worked and he stared hard at the lights on the tree. "That means a lot to me."

"You'll find a special gift from me and the rest

of us in Baltimore. We thought you might like your own set of our family pictures of our mother. She loved you to her dying day. I know this for a fact. I wish more than anything she could have met you. That she could have come on this trip with us. She would have been so pleased with your family. So very proud of you."

Ben said nothing. His nod of thanks was enough. "I know we need to get to the church in a bit, but there's something I was hoping you could help me with."

"Absolutely." She was surprised when Ben strolled to the little end table by the couch and pulled out its drawer. There lay a small worn book of Psalms she recognized and a delicate pearl-set cross. "This had to have been Mom's."

"I've always figured it was. It came with me when I was adopted." Ben scooped up the book and cross and, fighting emotions, nodded once. "It's good to know for sure."

"Mom's faith was deeply important to her. She probably gave you this because it was the thing that meant the most to her." Debra struggled with the memories of her mother's harsher side. Now she understood her mom's sharp edge had come from a pain that knew no measure or end. Giving away a newborn infant, so helpless and precious, had to have broken Millie down to the quick of her soul.

Poor Mom, she thought, wishing she'd known. Wishing her mother would have trusted her enough. Maybe, somehow, there would have been a way to help her. Now the best thing she could do was to face Ben, her mother's secret and her feelings over her mother's shortcomings with love. Wasn't that at the heart of faith, after all? God's love for us. Our love for Him. Our love for one another. She was more of a believer than she'd realized.

When she finally spoke, her voice trembled. "Mom and her sister, Rosalind, had these identical books and crosses. A gift from their grandmother. Rosalind left hers to Mia. Mom never said where hers went and it wasn't among any of her things after she passed."

Debra felt her world changing around her and there was nothing she wanted to do to stop it. The shields she'd kept around her heart were cracking forever. The peace she'd lost long-ago came back to her like a rush into her soul.

Debra held out her hand to her brother, her mother's first born. "It's almost time for the Christmas Eve service. Let's go. I can't wait to hear Olivia sing."

* * *

In the dark Tiny Blessings offices, Ross checked the face of his watch. The illuminated hands told him they'd been in place for nearly two hours. Any later and they would miss the Christmas Eve Service. He thought of his wife, who would be under the watchful eyes of his sister, Trista, and the assistant director of these offices, Eric Pellegrino. She was safe, he knew. His son was safe. That's what mattered.

Still, he wished this were over. He prayed for Douglas Matthews to make his move so they could wrap this up. So the man could pay for his crimes. For Wendy Kates's death. For Lynda Matthews's treatment. And, most importantly to Ross, for the attack against his family. Matthews had made this personal.

And so had he. His muscles protested as he waited in the dark beside Zach and two other detectives. Zach was on his radio. Ross hoped this was it.

"Word is he's pulled up in the alley." Zach sounded steady as he hefted his weapon. They were all in Kevlar vests, locked and loaded. Ross owed his buddy big-time for letting him be part of the takedown. "We've got him on video, so let's do this right. Take our time. Let's get ready, boys."

Ross was more than ready. He was so anxious for justice that he could taste it. He waited while his heart raced, until he heard the faintest sound. A footstep outside the back door. Then a quiet thump, thump.

Matthews was bumping the lock, Ross realized. It was a technique burglars used and it worked on most types of dead bolts. Apparently Matthews used his money to do more than pay to keep his secrets hidden. He bought everything—skill, information, you name it—he needed.

But the one thing he couldn't buy was his innocence. He was about to go down for a long list of charges that would stick. There wasn't a defense attorney that could get him off, no matter what he charged. Satisfied, Ross felt the tension in the room ratchet up a notch.

The door slowly swung open, letting in a faint fall of ambient light from the alleyway. There was Matthews, a black shadow against that light, wearing a ski mask to hide his face, but there was no mistaking the expensive Italian shoes he wore or his muttered curse as he debated his first move. Then he set the small bag he carried onto the edge of the desk and tilted his head back to look at the ceiling.

"I want to burn this place to the ground once

and for all," Matthews muttered angrily. "Those sprinklers have got to go first."

The man intended to set the offices on fire again. In the dark at Ross's side, Zach gave the sign and the team moved. The lights flashed on to illuminate the police unit, their rifles aimed at Douglas.

"Douglas Matthews, you are under arrest for sabotage and attempted murder. Put your hands in the air," Zach called out as his men moved closer. The masked man gaped at them in astonishment. "Coleman, read him his rights."

Ross marched forward and yanked off the ski mask. He wanted to see the expression on Matthews's face. He wasn't disappointed. Pure hatred twisted the talk-show host's mouth and deadened his eyes. "This is the real face of Douglas Matthews."

"You." Douglas spewed venom as he was cuffed. "I can't believe this. You ruined everything."

"No, you did that yourself, Matthews." Ross tossed the mask on the closest desk and watched with disdain as the man spit fury at the officers. "Say goodbye to your fame, your fortune and your freedom."

"Well, Ross, we did it." Zach grinned at

him. "We got our man and the victims will get their justice."

"I intend to make sure of it." Ross had all the evidence the district attorney needed to make the charges stick. And more, he thought when he remembered Wendy Kates. He gave thanks right then and there that his wife and son had not met a similar fate.

It was over. The reputation of Tiny Blessings would be restored and his beloved Kelly was safe. When he thought of his wife and their son, tender love overwhelmed him. They were a blessing he would always cherish, protect and take good care of.

"You have just enough time to get your family to Christmas Eve services," Zach said. "I'll take things from here."

"Thanks, buddy." There would be more work to do to tie up this case, but it could wait. His family—and his love for them—could not.

He headed out into the crisp night and watched while Matthews was caged in the back of a patrol car. Then he turned his thoughts toward home and the happy holidays he would have with his wife and son.

When the Christmas Eve service ended with a final prayer, Jonah had never been so relieved.

He'd done his best to concentrate on the program and on his dad's sermon, but he couldn't. The peace and hope and faith offered tonight hurt like an abscess. He'd gotten good at keeping his wounds tucked away. Until Debra.

She made him feel in ways he had vowed never to experience again. She tempted him with life and love and dreams fulfilled when it was the last thing he could ever deserve. He'd failed his team. His betrayal felt enormous against the contrast of hope and worship and faith on this holy night.

His every sense was tuned to Debra, who was far behind him and on the other side of the church, seated with Ben and his family. Knowing she was there rubbed like salt in a mortal wound and it stung so much he felt the heat behind his eyes. He could not bear it.

So he refused to look in her direction. Even when the congregation shuffled down the aisles and the murmur of talk and movements and children calling out surrounded him, he kept his gaze down. He headed for the front where he could make himself useful removing the nativity-scene props.

But as he worked, he couldn't focus on the task at hand. Thoughts about the woman he loved plagued him, for he did love her. More than he'd allowed himself to believe. He felt like a shadow that did not deserve light and he could not purge the image from his mind of Debra's touch trying to comfort him. Debra's voice full of love for him. Debra's patient steadfast understanding even after he'd driven her away.

If he could let this guilt and grief go, *if* he could find a way to wrestle down this suffocating sense of failure, he'd ruined every chance with her. There was no way she would forgive him after what he'd done to her and what he'd said. He couldn't blame her.

He was so lost in his turmoil, he didn't hear the footsteps coming up behind him until it was too late. He wasn't surprised to hear Ben's voice calling to him. "Jonah, I got something for you."

Please, Lord, Jonah prayed. *Don't let Debra be with him.* He'd hurt her. He was hurting too much to be strong enough to hold it together. He turned slowly to find Ben alone, holding a small wrapped gift in one hand.

"I promised Debra I'd deliver this to you after she'd left town."

"Debra's gone?" The air stalled in his lungs. Something stronger than grief hit him like an artillery shell, something more permanent than regret. It was the reality of love lost. The one chance for happiness he'd come across since he'd been back from Iraq. "She's driving home tonight?"

"No, I meant she's left for the inn tonight. She's leaving for Baltimore in the morning. I was supposed to deliver this after she'd left town."

Jonah took the gift wrapped in red foil paper with a fancy gold ribbon. It had the weight and size of a DVD.

"I've noticed what's been going on between you and my sister."

"Nothing happened."

Ben jammed his fists into his coat pockets. "I was hoping something would."

Nothing ever could. Regret shattered him and he wished this was something he could take to prayer. He wanted peace. He wanted to lay this burden down. But how? It would not be noble. It would not be right. He could not simply forget and push aside what had happened over there.

He wished—he prayed—that he could.

Ben shrugged. "Merry Christmas, Jonah."

It was all he could do to get the words out to say the same. After Ben walked away to join his wife and kids waiting for him at the back of the church, Jonah was left with Debra's gift in hand and the endless love for her in his broken heart. His fingers were already ripping at the paper before he'd made the conscious decision to open the present. He settled onto the front pew and parted the thick red paper to see the title of the movie staring up at him. His hands began to tremble.

"It's a wonderful life." Dad's words seemed to come out of nowhere.

He'd been trying not to feel, not to breathe, not to feel anything, and for what? He failed completely. "It's the movie I couldn't find for Mom."

"I wasn't talking about the movie, son." John Fraser looked weary as he settled onto the pew. "I'm talking about you. You've been sorely troubled since your discharge and I've been patient. I've told your mother we need to give you time. But it seems to me that you're about to run out of it."

Jonah crumpled the paper into a ball with one fist. The truth felt like a razor searing deep into his flesh. "I can't talk about it, Dad. All the time in the world can't change the past."

"But it's your present at stake. Your future. Anyone with eyes can see you're sweet on that nice lady."

Had it been that obvious? Jonah didn't try to deny what was true. "I'm more than sweet on her, Dad. I love her."

"Then why aren't you with her?"

"It's not that simple." Jonah thought of the men he'd let down. "She wouldn't want me if she knew."

Dad was silent for a while. The church had emptied. The silence echoed around them. "Maybe it's time you let go of whatever happened over there. What? You looked surprised. I watched you come back a different man than the one who left here for boot camp. Don't get me wrong. I'm proud of how you endured hardship and danger to serve this country. But I can see the cost."

Torture. That's what this was. Jonah rubbed his hand over his face. "Why does everyone assume I did good over there?"

"Because we all know the man you are. Maybe it's time you talked about it. Tell me what horrible thing you did."

"I lived," he choked out, ashamed, endlessly, mercilessly ashamed. This time, the horrors of war didn't wait for dreams. The images flashed before his eyes. The men he'd vowed to fight and die beside. The men who'd died without him.

"Do you think it was your duty to die with your men?" Dad's hand settled on his shoulder.

Unable to speak, he nodded. What would his father think of him now? "I was hit bad, but not as bad as everyone else. I don't know why I lived. I shouldn't have."

"Son, it's not your job to question. You have to trust that God knows what He's doing. Maybe He's not finished with working His good through you."

"But the others—"

"You must never forget them. But God preserved your life. You have to accept this gift and live it. You cannot turn your back on the blessing God has given you. He chose you, Jonah."

"For what?" He could not imagine what he had to offer.

"Maybe to remember what happened over there. What you and your men did and the difference you made. When you were younger, you wanted to write a book one day, remember?"

"I see where you're going with this, Dad, but still. I can't accept—" He felt so lost. Could this be the way out? The only honor in surviving would be to bring the memories of those men with him. Maybe his dad had a good idea.

And what about Debra? Remembering how

she'd looked with the snow in her hair and the soft glow of the streetlights hazing around her like a dream brought back their evening walk down Christmas Lane. How alive he'd felt. Full of heart.

Her love for him had made the pain of the past recede. Could his love for her do the same? "I don't want the past to destroy the best thing that's happened to me. But I don't know what to do."

"Then I'll show you. Let's pray together. I'm certain God doesn't want you to hurt so much. This was never in your hands, Jonah. It always was and always will be in His."

Grateful and soul-weary, Jonah bowed his head, ready to lay down his burden at last.

Chapter Fourteen

Christmas morning. It was with a heavy but wiser heart that Debra took a look around her room at the bed-and-breakfast for anything she'd forgotten, but it looked as if she'd packed everything. Her suitcases were already loaded in the back of the SUV and Mia's sat by the open adjoining door. There was nothing left to do but to take it, turn off the radio and go.

As she reached for the radio, the instrumental Christmas carol came to an end. An announcer's grave voice began reporting the news. "Last night, police arrested Douglas Matthews for sabotage and attempted murder in his efforts to thwart Ross Van Zandt's investigation into the murder of Wendy Kates. A press conference is scheduled—"

She clicked the button, and the radio fell

silent. Douglas Matthews. He certainly had fooled a lot of people with his golden-boy-does-good facade. She remembered how he'd behaved outside the diner and felt sad for the peoples' lives he'd damaged or destroyed.

Debra took a sip of steaming coffee from her travel mug. Mia, kneeling in prayer, whispered earnestly, as if with all her heart. Such high hopes. The girl had refused to give up her belief that God had more in store for them on this trip—although there was only a few more minutes left for God to work it all out.

"Amen," Mia whispered faithfully, lifted her head and opened her eyes. Her fingers remained clasped. "Oh, hi, Mom. Do we have to go now?"

"We'll be late to Christmas dinner if we don't get on our way."

"I don't want that." She rose, looking very festive in her Christmas-green cable-knit sweater and black jeans. Her fashionable suede boots matched the jacket she'd chosen. "Do you know what I really want, Mom?"

"To come back and visit your uncle Ben and his family soon?"

"Yes, but I already knew we were going to do that." Mia paused over buttoning her coat. Her dark hair fell like satin, framing her innocent heart-shaped face. "It's something else that I want more than anything."

"To not go to the Stanton School. I know." Debra held out her hand. "C'mon, kid, let's you and I hit the road."

"Mom, I'm not a kid anymore." Mia slid her palm against Debra's and clasped their fingers together. "I'm a teenager now."

"I've noticed something like that." Debra couldn't help smiling as she checked around Mia's room—nothing forgotten here, either—and followed her daughter into the main bedroom. The wide window looked out over trees flocked white with snow. Phone lines and rooftops and every surface were frosted with a fresh icinglike sweetness.

It *is* a wonderful life, Debra decided. She asked Mia to carry the cup of coffee for her as she snagged the suitcase's handle on the way out the door. They had everything. There was nothing else to do but leave.

Because it was so early, they were quiet as they descended the staircase. Debra stopped to haul the keys out of her jacket pocket and tuck them into the little key-collection box for the morning clerk to find.

"Mom." Mia was taking one last look around at the garlands and wreaths and the dark Christmas tree standing solemnly in the corner. "You were wrong about me not wanting to go to school. I mean, I don't want to go, sure, but that's not what I want more than anything."

And what would that be, Debra wondered, unable to ask the question. Her heart hurt too much with what could not be. A forever love with Jonah. An adorable little bookshop. Having more children. All that seemed lost now. But she didn't feel down. Maybe God had something marvelous in store for her somewhere in the future. She would hold out hope for that.

Debra reached for the doorknob, but didn't get a chance to turn it.

Mia was talking again. "I want you to be happy, Mom. Really happy. I've never seen you as filled with joy as you've been here in Chestnut Grove with Jonah. Do you think we could see him before we go? So we could maybe invite him to New Year's Eve, too? Uncle Ben and Aunt Leah are coming and I thought—"

"Jonah isn't interested in getting married to me." It was the truth, a fact, that was all. She could not let it sound like anything more. She would not allow herself to feel the jagged edges of her freshly broken dream. "Ben will bring the rest of the furniture when he comes for New

Year's. You could call Jonah and thank him then."

"Mom." Mia no longer looked like a little girl, but a younger woman who could understand. "I'm sorry. I know you really liked him."

"I loved him." Debra shrugged as if it were not the end of the world. And it felt like it was not. There was no fix and no cure but maybe time would heal the pain. She didn't know. But she had Mia—the best blessing of all. "I've been thinking about that school you don't like."

"I don't like it because I'm away from you, Mom."

"That's why I don't like it, either."

"Really? You don't mean—" Hope lit Mia's face. She paused, as if she were afraid to say the words.

"I would like you to finish out the year. But I'll come visit more and we'll zip you home for as many weekends as you want."

"Mom! That's the best Christmas present ever. Do you really, really mean it?"

"Yes, and we'll choose next year's school together."

"But what about tradition?"

"It's not as important as being with you. I think Grandmother Millie would understand."

"Oh, thank you, Mom!" Mia launched herself at Debra. Her hug was one-hundred-percent pure glee. Good thing the travel mug had a spill-proof top.

Overcome with love, Debra pressed a kiss to her daughter's forehead. "You're growing up on me, baby. You're not my little girl anymore."

"But we'll always be best friends, right, Mom?"

"Right." Tears of gratitude blurred her vision as she followed her daughter to the door.

Thank you, Lord, she couldn't help sending a little prayer heavenward. *Thanks for bringing us back together.*

"Mom," Mia said on the other side of the front door, "look who's here. It's Jonah."

Jonah? Debra stepped out into the bitter chill of the early morning. There, straight ahead of them, leaning against their SUV parked in the loading zone, stood a tall, powerful-looking man in a parka, jeans and boots. It was his smile she didn't know she longed for until she saw it. Her spirit rejoiced simply from having him near.

And why was he here? That momentary joy ebbed as she sensibly reminded herself that there was a perfectly rational explanation for Jonah's presence. He'd come to say goodbye and nothing more.

She took the stairs slowly, taking care on the

snowy steps. It was so early, no one had cleared away the falling snow yet, and she was thankful because it gave her something to think about as Mia ran ahead, careful to keep her voice low in the morning stillness, and chat excitedly with Jonah.

Keep your eyes down, she told herself as the suitcase bumped on the steps, and don't let your broken heart show. She'd held it together this long. Surely she could manage a few more minutes. The icy wind and snow battered her face. Seeing him hurt like a freshly cut wound, but maybe this was better. She could say goodbye with her dignity intact and end this thing between them on a positive note. She loved him. She knew beyond all doubt she would always love him.

"Let me get that." Jonah's voice. Jonah's gloved hand closing over hers on the suitcase's handle. Jonah blocking her from the brunt of the storm.

Jonah. Her one true love. Debra froze, paralyzed in place as he gently took charge of the suitcase. His dark eyes met hers and, in that perfect moment, there was no rejection, no lost chances and no shadowed pain. Only her love for him blazing in her soul. Only the same brand of love reflected back at her in his gaze.

He broke away, leaving her motionless in the middle of the stairs, glossed with snow and iced with cold. Had she imaged it? she wondered as he tromped away and stowed the last suitcase in the back with the others and closed the back hatch. Hope began to rise within her.

This sacred morning, frosted with white perfection felt like the right place for wishes to come true. For love to prevail. Her boots carried her forward in the soft cushion of downy snow. She could have been walking on clouds.

"I couldn't let you leave without your Christmas present." Jonah pulled a small package from his jacket pocket. His hand trembled a little as he held it out.

Debra could only stare at the gift wrapped in white-and-gold wrapping perched in the center of Jonah's outstretched palm. The present was no larger than her cell phone. While she'd heard the cliché good things come in small packages, she sensibly told herself that this was a token, nothing more, but merely a gift to exchange because she had given him one. Why, then, did her hopes lift as high as a prayer?

"Open it, Mom." Mia's eyes were bright with expectation. "I want to see what it is."

Jonah padded closer, so close only the falling

snow came between them. "Go on. I was up half the night making this."

"You shouldn't have gone to so much trouble."

"It was no trouble because it was for you. Go on. Open it. Please?"

She could not say no to him, but she feared he was asking too much. There was a plea on his rugged face she did not understand, so she tugged off her gloves and stowed them in her jacket pocket. The cold nipped her fingertips as she picked at the tape on one end of the package. The paper came away to reveal a delicate wooden box, like a tiny jewel case.

"It's exquisite," she breathed, knowing he'd made it, incredibly, himself. The wood grain was red oak, she guessed, with inlaid cherry-wood rose petals, held in a cup of raised, carved leaves. "I've never seen anything so lovely."

"Wait until you see what's inside."

She was intrigued. The box was small and flat. What could it hold? She didn't think he would give her a piece of jewelry, but it was the only thing she could guess the box might hold.

When she lifted the lid, there was a silver door key inside lying on a bed of gold velvet. Just a key. Nothing more. What did it mean? She looked to him for an answer, but he only gestured toward his truck parked and idling behind her SUV.

"It's a short drive. Do you want to come with me?"

Yes, her heart answered. Those broken dreams had taken shape again and she began to wish for that future she'd gotten a glimpse of—the one with Jonah in it.

The streets were empty this time of the morning, the roads shining with an icy gloss. He concentrated on his driving, or maybe he was thinking hard, and he didn't speak until he turned left and it was clear he was taking her to the carpentry shop.

Her hopes sank back down to the ground. The key could not be a significant gift. She was still puzzled. Still hopeful. She straightened her spine, pressing her back against the leather seat and managed to keep an indifferent look on her face. That might be best for whatever lay ahead.

Jonah pulled against the curb halfway down the block. "Mia, do you mind waiting here where it's warm? I need to speak to your mom outside."

"Sure. You talk to her all you want." Her wide smile said it all.

Mia and her high hopes, Debra thought as she unlatched herself from the seat and opened the truck door with clumsy fingers. Jonah was there before her boots hit the snowy sidewalk. His hand cupped her elbow. Love lit his face.

Love. Not torture. Not sadness. Not grief. He was no longer the man turning away from her and pushing her away. He no longer looked like a man with nothing to offer.

He cradled her face in his hands. "First off, can you forgive me for the way I treated you? I'm sorry. Debra, I'm so, so sorry."

"I know you are." How could she forget how tortured and grief-stricken he'd looked? "I know you were hurting, Jonah."

"That doesn't excuse it. I was trying to spare you more pain. I wasn't ready." He looked agonized in a different way now. "I thought you wouldn't understand what happened to me over there. That you would think I'd let my men down. I didn't feel I could deserve someone as amazing and precious as you."

"Of course I understand and there's nothing to forgive." Dear Jonah. Of course he hadn't let his men down. He deserved all the happiness in the world. What a good man he was. Strong of character and even stronger at heart. Endless love for him welled up from her soul, filling her until she brimmed with happiness. With hope. "I know the man you are, Jonah. The man I love."

"Love? I'm sure relieved you said that. Because I love you, too. With all I am and all I have." He paused, his throat worked as he gathered the right words. "Debra, will you marry me?"

What? Had she heard him right? Debra stared at him for a full beat. It was the key that had thrown her. Now he was offering her a ring? Tears filled her eyes, blurring him, and she let them fall. Happy tears trailed down her face as she heard another voice ring out from behind her.

"Yes! She'll marry you, Jonah. I know she wants to."

Debra wasn't surprised to see her daughter leaning out the window, beaming with happiness. "It's not polite to eavesdrop, kid."

"Yeah, I know, but you need my help, Mom." Mia clasped her hands together prayerfully. "Say yes, 'cause I think I know what that key is for."

Debra hadn't realized where they were standing. Jonah hadn't randomly pulled over along the street. Snow hazed the scene, and when the big man blocking her view stepped aside, she recognized the little bookshop. The sale sign in the window was gone. She looked down at the key in the box in her hand.

"Surely this can't be for—" Her throat closed on the words. "You couldn't have bought—"

"The bookstore is yours."

"Mine? But—"

"Shh." He brushed away her tears with the pads of his thumbs. "Sorry, there will be no excuses, no protests, no way out. This is a gift from my heart to yours. Because your dreams are my dreams. Because you are my dream."

"You are my dream, too. You make me melt. All my defenses. All my practical, sensible plans." Her beautiful eyes sparkled up at him full of love. Endless love. "You make me want everything."

And because he knew exactly what she meant, because he wanted everything with her, too, he kissed her tenderly and true. Love swept through the places within him that had been full of hurt and regret. With faith in his future, he asked her one more time. "Say yes. Marry me. Please."

"Yes. Yes. Yes."

Exactly the word he needed to hear. A whole new future opened up to him, built on the ashes of the old. Where there had been regret, he now had forgiveness. Grief had turned to hope. He could see their life together as man and wife. He'd work at the carpentry shop. She would have her bookshop. They'd get a house and fill it with happiness and devotion and more children.

"I will love you for the rest of my life," he promised.

"And into forever," she added, and they sealed their vows with a kiss. Snow fell like blessings over them as Mia punched the air, a complete believer in the power of prayer.

Epilogue

Two weeks before Christmas, one year later.

Debra squinted through the mellow afternoon sunshine at her husband perched on the ladder hanging the last of the Christmas decorations. Icicle lights dripped from the eaves of their recently purchased Tudor—formerly Pamela Lansbury's gracious house. Snow graced the roof and frosted the lamp-lit windows. Already it was their beloved home.

"How does it look?" Jonah called over his shoulder.

"Great. Mia is going to be pleased."

"Then my work here is done. I'm coming down."

The wind chose that moment to gust, bringing with it the chill and scent of coming snow. Debra shivered and wrapped her sash around her thickening waist a little more tightly. Pretty soon she'd have to go shopping for maternity clothes, including a warm winter coat. She was due in May, but the little girl she carried was making herself known. She pressed her hand gently against the swell of her stomach.

"You okay?" Jonah was pure concern as he ambled toward her.

"She's moving. She's going to be an active one."

"I've already picked out where I'm putting up the basketball hoop, just in case she's athletic like me." Jonah wrapped his arms around her, sheltering her, drawing her close. "This time last year, did you think we would wind up married and happy?"

"No. A year ago, I'd just driven into town and was not looking forward to what was ahead." Debra lay her cheek on Jonah's chest, comforted by his strong heartbeat. "If you would have told me in twelve short months I would have quit my job, sold my house, be running a bookstore and have a bought a home in Chestnut Grove with you, I wouldn't have believed it."

"What about the part about marrying me? You left that important part out."

"Oh, well, I thought you were handsome right away." She tilted her face up to let him kiss her sweetly. "And I thought you were the most wonderful man I'd met. So, no. I might have believed that part. I feel as if God brought me here to meet you, the love of my life."

"You are the love of my life, too. I will love you forever." His hand cupped her jaw. The pad of his thumb rubbed gently against the side of her face. So much everlasting love shone in his eyes, it was without measure and without end.

Just as her love was for him.

The sound of a diesel engine broke the stillness down the street. Air brakes sounded as wheels squeaked to a stop. Debra didn't have to look down the lane. "Mia's home from school."

"I'd best plug in the lights. We'll surprise her." Jonah moved away, his burden and shadows gone now that his book was finished and awaiting publication. Jonah bent down, hit the switch and the lights blazed on in a twinkle of pure white.

Mia's boots thudded on the sidewalk. "I can't believe this! You did the lights without me."

"But we're waiting for your final approval," Debra pointed out. "How was school today?"

"Fabulous. I've got that debate-team thing this weekend, don't forget. Plus, I'm practically late to Christmas- pageant practice." Mia rolled her eyes. She was now a tall, lively, lovely fourteen-year-old, who was happy and thriving at the local high school. "So much to do, so little time. Mom, are you coming to watch?"

"Of course. I'm sure they can get along at the bookshop without me for another few hours."

"Great!" Mia tromped up the walk, books on her arm and a heavy backpack slung over one shoulder. She paused to exchange words with Jonah about the lights before she disappeared through the front door.

Thank you, Lord. Debra couldn't help the prayer of thanks that rose up from her soul. Life was good. Mia was happy. Jonah was at peace. Her marriage was perfection.

"It's snowing." Her husband held out his hand to her. Tiny crystalline flakes drifted from the partly cloudy sky. "C'mon, beautiful. Let me make my girls a batch of hot chocolate before we head off to choir practice."

Yes, her life was definitely wonderful. Full of faith, she let her husband escort her up the steps.

As she went to shut the door, the wind gusted

through the twinkle lights. The snow fell like grace at her feet and she knew this Christmas, her first one as Jonah's wife, was going to be another holiday to remember.

* * * * *

Dear Reader,

Thank you so much for picking up *A Holiday to Remember*. I hope you enjoyed reading Debra's story as much as I enjoyed writing it. I am very grateful to Steeple Hill Books for allowing me to tell this story of a strong woman, a single mother, who is managing her life successfully and yet has not found personal happiness. She meets Jonah Fraser, who is also unable to find peace and forgiveness because of his past. I hope that Debra and Jonah's journey to find healing speaks to your life, too.

Wishing you grace and peace this holiday season,

Jillian Hart

QUESTIONS FOR DISCUSSION

1. At the beginning of the story when Debra arrives in town to meet with her brother, she is struggling hard not to be pessimistic and expect the worst. What does it say about Debra? Have you ever struggled with pessimism?

2. What is Jonah's first impression of Debra? As he comes to know her, what aspects of her character does he come to admire?

3. Debra found herself a single mother at a relatively young age and it caused a rift with her mother. How has this affected her? How does that keep her from trusting others?

4. What do Jonah and Debra have in common? How does this bring them closer together?

5. How have Jonah's experiences as a marine made him the right man for Debra? What aspects of his character does she come to admire?

6. How important are the themes of trust and forgiveness in this story? What role does the Christmas season play?

7. How does knowing Jonah change Debra? How does he help her come to terms with the problems she had with her mother?

8. How does God's leading bring Debra and Jonah together?

9. How does Debra find her faith in God again?

10. What role does Mia's hopeful, faithful outlook play in the story?

LOVE INSPIRED HISTORICAL

*Powerful, engaging stories of romance,
adventure and faith set in the past—
when life was simpler
and faith played a major role
in everyday lives.*

*Turn the page for a sneak preview of
HOMESPUN BRIDE
by Jillian Hart.
Love Inspired Historical—love and faith
throughout the ages.
A brand-new line from Steeple Hill Books
launching this February!*

There was something about the young woman—
something he couldn't put his finger on. He'd
hardly glanced at her when he'd hauled her from
the family sleigh, but now he took a longer look
through the veil of falling snow.

For a moment her silhouette, her size and her
movements all reminded him of Noelle. How
about that. Noelle, his frozen heart reminded
him with a painful squeeze, had been his first—
and only—love.

It couldn't be her, he reasoned, since she was
married and probably a mother by now. She'd
be safe in town, living snug in one of the finest
houses in the county instead of riding along the
country roads in a storm. Still, curiosity nibbled
at him, and he plowed through the knee-deep

snow. Snow was falling faster now, and yet somehow through the thick downfall his gaze seemed to find her.

She was fragile, a delicate bundle of wool—and snow clung to her hood and scarf and cloak like a shroud, making her tough to see. She'd been just a little bit of a thing when he'd lifted her from the sleigh, and his only thought at the time had been to get both women out of danger. Now something chewed at his memory. He couldn't quite figure out what, but he could feel it in his gut.

The woman was talking on as she unwound her niece's veil. "We were tossed about dreadfully. You're likely bruised and broken from root to stem. I've never been so terrified. All I could do was pray over and over and think of you, my dear." Her words warmed with tenderness. "What a greater nightmare for you."

"We're fine. All's well that ends well," the niece insisted.

Although her voice was muffled by the thick snowfall, his step faltered. There *was* something about her voice, something familiar in the gentle resonance of her alto. Now he could see the top part of her face, due to her loosened scarf. Her eyes—they were a startling, flawless emerald green.

Whoa, there. He'd seen that perfect shade of green before—and long ago. Recognition speared through his midsection, but he already knew she was his Noelle even before the last layer of the scarf fell away from her face.

His Noelle, just as lovely and dear, was now blind and veiled with snow. His first love. The woman he'd spent years and thousands of miles trying to forget. Hard to believe that there she was suddenly right in front of him. He'd heard about the engagement announcement a few years back, and he'd known in returning to live in Angel Falls that he'd have to run into her eventually.

He just didn't figure it would be so soon and like this.

Seeing her again shouldn't make him feel as if he'd been hit in the chest with a cannonball. The shock was wearing off, he realized, the same as when you received a hard blow. First off, you were too stunned to feel it. Then the pain began to settle in, just a hint, and then rushing in until it was unbearable. Yep, that was the word to describe what was happening inside his rib cage. A pain worse than a broken bone beat through him.

Best get the sleigh righted, the horse hitched back up and the women home. But it was all he could to do turn his back as he took his mustang by the bridle. The palomino pinto gave him a snort and shook his head, sending the snow on his golden mane flying.

I know how you feel, Sunny, Thad thought. Judging by the look of things, it would be a long time until they had a chance to get in out of the cold.

He'd do best to ignore the women, especially Noelle, and to get to the work needin' to be done. He gave the sleigh a shove, but the vehicle was wedged against the snow-covered brush banking the river. Not that he'd put a lot of weight on the Lord over much these days, but Thad had to admit it was a close call. Almost eerie how he'd caught them just in time. It did seem providential. Had they gone only a few feet more, gravity would have done the trick and pulled the sleigh straight into the frigid, fast waters of Angel River and plummeted them directly over the tallest falls in the territory.

Thad squeezed his eyes shut. He couldn't stand to think of Noelle tossed into that river, fighting the powerful current along with the ice chunks. There would have been no way to have pulled her from the river in time. Had he been a few minutes slower in coming after

them or if Sunny hadn't been so swift, there
would have been no way to save her. To fate,
to the Lord or to simple chance, he was
grateful.

Some tiny measure of tenderness in his
chest, like a fire long banked, sputtered to life.
His tenderness for her, still there, after so much
time and distance. How about that.

Since the black gelding was a tad calmer now
that the sound of the train had faded off into the
distance, Thad rehitched him to the sleigh but
secured the driving reins to his saddle horn. He
used the two horses working together to free the
sleigh and get it realigned toward the road.

The older woman looked uncertain about
getting back into the vehicle. With the way that
black gelding of theirs was twitchy and wild-
eyed, he didn't blame her. "Don't worry,
ma'am, I'll see you two ladies home."

"Th-that would be very good of you, sir. I'm
rather shaken up. I've half a mind to walk the
entire mile home, except for my dear niece."

Noelle. He wouldn't let his heart react to her.
All that mattered was doing right by her—and
that was one thing that hadn't changed. He
came around to help the aunt into the sleigh and
after she was safely seated, turned toward
Noelle. Her scarf had slid down to reveal the

curve of her face, the slope of her nose and the rosebud smile of her mouth.

What had happened to her? How had she lost her sight? Sadness filled him for her blindness and for what could have been between them, once. He thought about saying something to her, so she would know who he was, but what good would that do? The past was done and over. Only the emptiness of it remained.

"Thank you so much, sir." She turned toward the sound of his step and smiled in his direction. If she, too, wondered who he was, she gave no real hint of it.

He didn't expect her to. Chances were she hardly remembered him, and if she did, she wouldn't think too well of him. She would never know what good wishes he wanted for her as he took her gloved hand. The layers of wool and leather and sheepskin lining between his hand and hers didn't stop that tiny flame of tenderness for her in his chest from growing a notch.

He looked into her eyes, into Noelle's eyes, the woman he'd loved truly so long ago, knowing she did not recognize him. Could not see him or sense him, even at heart. She smiled at him as if he were the Good Samaritan she thought he was as he helped her settle onto the seat.

Love was an odd thing, he realized as he backed away. Once, their love had been an emotion felt so strong and pure and true that he would have vowed on his very soul that nothing could tarnish nor diminish their bond. But time had done that simply, easily, and they stood now as strangers.

* * * * *

Don't miss this deeply moving
Love Inspired Historical story about a
young woman in 1883 Montana who reunites
with an old beau and soon discovers that
love is the greatest blessing of all.

HOMESPUN BRIDE
by Jillian Hart
available February 2008.
And also look for
THE BRITON
by Catherine Palmer,
About a medieval lady who battles for her
family legacy—and finds true love.

Love Inspired®

SUSPENSE

RIVETING INSPIRATIONAL ROMANCE

Watch for our new series of
edge-of-your-seat suspense novels.
These contemporary tales
of intrigue and romance
feature Christian characters
facing challenges to their faith...
and their lives!

Steeple
Hill®

Visit:
www.SteepleHill.com